Charles Stuart Calverley

Verses and Translations

Charles Stuart Calverley

Verses and Translations

Reprint of the original, first published in 1871.

1st Edition 2022 | ISBN: 978-3-36812-653-7

Verlag (Publisher): Outlook Verlag GmbH, Zeilweg 44, 60439 Frankfurt, Deutschland
Vertretungsberechtigt (Authorized to represent): E. Roepke, Zeilweg 44, 60439 Frankfurt, Deutschland
Druck (Print): Books on Demand GmbH, In de Tarpen 42, 22848 Norderstedt, Deutschland

VERSES

AND

TRANSLATIONS.

VERSES

AND

TRANSLATIONS

By C. S. C.

FOURTH EDITION, REVISED.

CAMBRIDGE:

DEIGHTON, BELL, AND CO.

LONDON: BELL AND DALDY.

1871

CONTENTS.

CONTENTS.

VISIONS.

"She was a phantom," &c.

IN lone Glenartney's thickets lies couched the
  lordly stag,
The dreaming terrier's tail forgets its customary
  wag;
And plodding ploughmen's weary steps insensibly
  grow quicker,
As broadening casements light them on toward
  home, or home-brewed liquor.

It is in brief the evening—that pure and pleasant
  time,
When stars break into splendour, and poets into
  rhyme;

B

When in the glass of Memory the forms of loved
    ones shine—
And when, of course, Miss Goodchild's is prominent
    in mine.

Miss Goodchild!—Julia Goodchild!—how graciously
    you smiled
Upon my childish passion once, yourself a fair-
    haired child:
When I was (no doubt) profiting by Dr. Crabb's
    instruction,
And sent those streaky lollipops home for your
    fairy suction!

"She wore" her natural "roses, the night when
    first we met"—
Her golden hair was gleaming 'neath the coercive
    net:
"Her brow was like the snawdrift," her step wɪ
    like Queen Mab's,

And gone was instantly the heart of every boy at
    Crabb's.

The parlour-boarder chasséed tow'rds her on graceful
    limb ;
The onyx deck'd his bosom—but her smiles were
    not for him :
With *me* she danced—till drowsily her eyes " began
    to blink,"
And *I* brought raisin wine, and said, " Drink, pretty
    creature, drink !"

And evermore, when winter comes in his garb of
    snows,
And the returning schoolboy is told how fast he
    grows ;
Shall I—with that soft hand in mine—enact ideal
    Lancers,
And dream I hear demure remarks, and make
    impassioned answers :—

I know that never, never may her love for me
    return—

At night I muse upon the fact with undisguised
    concern—

But ever shall I bless that day: I don't bless, as
    a rule,

The days I spent at "Dr. Crabb's Preparatory
    School."

And yet we too *may* meet again—(Be still, my
    throbbing heart!)

Now rolling years have weaned us from jam and
    raspberry-tart.

One night I saw a vision—'Twas when musk-
    roses bloom,

I stood—*we* stood—upon a rug, in a sumptuous
    dining-room:

One hand clasped hers—one easily reposed upon
    my hip—

And "BLESS YE!" burst abruptly from Mr. Goodchild's lip :

I raised my brimming eye, and saw in hers an
answering gleam—

My heart beat wildly—and I woke, and lo! it was
a dream.

GEMINI AND VIRGO.

SOME vast amount of years ago,
 Ere all my youth had vanish'd from me,
A boy it was my lot to know,
 Whom his familiar friends called Tommy.

I love to gaze upon a child;
 A young bud bursting into blossom;
Artless, as Eve yet unbeguiled,
 And agile as a young opossum:

And such was he. A calm-brow'd lad,
 Yet mad, at moments, as a hatter:
Why hatters as a race are mad
 I never knew, nor does it matter.

He was what nurses call a "limb";
  One of those small misguided creatures,
Who, tho' their intellects are dim,
  Are one too many for their teachers:

And, if you asked of him to say
  What twice 10 was, or 3 times 7,
He'd glance (in quite a placid way)
  From heaven to earth, from earth to heaven;

And smile, and look politely round,
  To catch a casual suggestion;
But make no effort to propound
  Any solution of the question.

And so not much esteemed was he
  Of the authorities: and therefore
He fraternized by chance with me,
  Needing a somebody to care for:

And three fair summers did we twain
　　Live (as they say) and love together;
And bore by turns the wholesome cane
　　Till our young skins became as leather:

And carved our names on every desk,
　　And tore our clothes, and inked our collars;
And looked unique and picturesque,
　　But not, it may be, model scholars.

We did much as we chose to do;
　　We'd never heard of Mrs. Grundy;
All the theology we knew
　　Was that we mightn't play on Sunday;

And all the general truths, that cakes
　　Were to be bought at four a penny,
And that excruciating aches
　　Resulted if we ate too many:

And seeing ignorance is bliss,
　And wisdom consequently folly,
The obvious result is this—
　That our two lives were very jolly.

At last the separation came.
　Real love, at that time, was the fashion;
And by a horrid chance, the same
　Young thing was, to us both, a passion.

Old Poser snorted like a horse:
　His feet were large, his hands were pimply,
His manner, when excited, coarse:—
　But Miss P. was an angel simply.

She was a blushing gushing thing;
　All—more than all—my fancy painted;
Once—when she helped me to a wing
　Of goose—I thought I should have fainted.

The people said that she was blue:

    But I was green, and loved her dearly.

She was approaching thirty-two;

    And I was then eleven, nearly.

I did not love as others do;

    (None ever did that I've heard tell of;)

My passion was a byword through

    The town she was, of course, the belle of:

Oh sweet—as to the toilworn man

    The far-off sound of rippling river;

As to cadets in Hindostan

    The fleeting remnant of their liver—

To me was ANNA; dear as gold

    That fills the miser's sunless coffers;

As to the spinster, growing old,

    The thought—the dream—that she had offers

I'd sent her little gifts of fruit;

  I'd written lines to her as Venus;

I'd sworn unflinchingly to shoot

  The man who dared to come between us:

And it was you, my Thomas, you,

  The friend in whom my soul confided,

Who dared to gaze on her—to do,

  I may say, much the same as I did.

One night, I *saw* him squeeze her hand;

  There was no doubt about the matter;

I said he must resign, or stand

  My vengeance—and he chose the latter.

We met, we 'planted' blows on blows:

  We fought as long as we were able:

My rival had a bottle-nose,

  And both my speaking eyes were sable,

When the school-bell cut short our strife.

   Miss P. gave both of us a plaister;

And in a week became the wife

   Of Horace Nibbs, the writing-master.

    *   *   *   *   *

I loved her then—I'd love her still,

   Only one must not love Another's:

But thou and I, my Tommy, will,

   When we again meet, meet as brothers.

It may be that in age one seeks

   Peace only: that the blood is brisker

In boys' veins, than in theirs whose cheeks

   Are partially obscured by whisker;

Or that the growing ages steal

   The memories of past wrongs from us.

But this is certain—that I feel

   Most friendly unto thee, oh Thomas!

And wheresoe'er we meet again,

  On this or that side the equator,

If I've not turned teetotaller then,

  And have wherewith to pay the waiter,

To thee I'll drain the modest cup,

  Ignite with thee the mild Havannah;

And we will waft, while liquoring up,

  Forgiveness to the heartless ANNA.

"There stands a city."

INGOLDSB?

YEAR by year do Beauty's daughters,
  In the sweetest gloves and shawls,
Troop to taste the Chattenham waters,
  And adorn the Chattenham balls.

'*Nulla non donanda lauru,*'
  Is that city: you could not,
Placing England's map before you,
  Light on a more favour'd spot.

If no clear translucent river
  Winds 'neath willow-shaded paths,
"Children and adults" may shiver
  All day in "Chalybeate baths":

And on every side the painter
  Looks on wooded vale and plain
And on fair hills, faint and fainter
  Outlined as they near the main.

There I met with him, my chosen
  Friend—the 'long' but not 'stern swell,'*
Faultless in his hats and hosen,
  Whom the Johnian lawns know well:—

Oh my comrade, ever valued!
  Still I see your festive face;
Hear you humming of "the gal you'd
  Left behind" in massive bass:

See you sit with that composure
  On the eeliest of hacks,
That the novice would suppose your
  Manly limbs encased in wax:

* "The kites know well the long stern swell
    That bids the Romans close."—MACAULAY.

Or anon, when evening lent her
  Tranquil light to hill and vale,
Urge, towards the table's centre,
  With unerring hand, the squail.

Ah delectablest of summers!
  How my heart—that "muffled drum"
Which ignores the aid of drummers—
  Beats, as back thy memories come!

O among the dancers peerless,
  Fleet of foot, and soft of eye!
Need I say to you that cheerless
  Must my days be till I die?

At my side she mashed the fragrant
  Strawberry; lashes soft as silk
Drooped o'er saddened eyes, when vagrant
  Gnats sought watery graves in milk:

Then we danced, we walked together;
  Talked—no doubt on trivial topics;
Such as Blondin, or the weather,
  Which "recalled us to the tropics."

But—O in the deuxtemps peerless,
  Fleet of foot, and soft of eye!—
Once more I repeat, that cheerless
  Shall my days be till I die.

And the lean and hungry raven,
  As he picks my bones, will start
To observe 'M. N.' engraven
  Neatly on my blighted heart.

STRIKING.

IT was a railway passenger,
　　And he lept out jauntilie.
"Now up and bear, thou stout portèr,
　　My two chattèls to me.

"Bring hither, bring hither my bag so red,
　　And portmanteau so brown:
(They lie in the van, for a trusty man
　　He labelled them London town:)

　　"And fetch me eke a cabman bold,
　　That I may be his fare, his fare;
And he shall have a good shilling,
If by two of the clock he do me bring
　　To the Terminus, Euston Square."

" Now,—so to thee the saints alway,

Good gentleman, give luck,—

As never a cab may I find this day,

For the cabman wights have struck:

And now, I wis, at the Red Post Inn,

Or else at the Dog and Duck,

Or at Unicorn Blue, or at Green Griffin,

The nut-brown ale and the fine old gin

Right pleasantly they do suck."

"Now rede me aright, thou stout portèr,

What were it best that I should do:

For woe is me, an' I reach not there

Or ever the clock strike two."

"I have a son, a lytel son;

Fleet is his foot as the wild roebuck's:

Give him a shilling, and eke a brown,

And he shall carry thy fardels down

To Euston, or half over London town,
    On one of the station trucks."

Then forth in a hurry did they twain fare,
The gent, and the son of the stout portèr,
Who fled like an arrow, nor turned a hair,
    Through all the mire and muck:
"A ticket, a ticket, sir clerk, I pray:
For by two of the clock must I needs away."
"That may hardly be," the clerk did say,
    "For indeed—the clocks have struck."

VOICES OF THE NIGHT.

"The tender Grace of a day that is dead."

THE dew is on the roses,
  The owl hath spread her wing;
And vocal are the noses
  Of peasant and of king:
"Nature" in short "reposes";
  But I do no such thing.

Pent in my lonesome study
  Here I must sit and muse;
Sit till the morn grows ruddy,
  Till, rising with the dews,
"Jeameses" remove the muddy
  Spots from their masters' shoes.

Yet are sweet faces flinging
  Their witchery o'er me here:
I hear sweet voices singing
  A song as soft, as clear,
As (previously to stinging)
  A gnat sings round one's ear.

Does Grace draw young Apollo's
  In blue mustachios still?
Does Emma tell the swallows
  How she will pipe and trill,
When, some fine day, she follows
  Those birds to the window-sill?

And oh! has Albert faded
  From Grace's memory yet?
Albert, whose "brow was shaded
  By locks of glossiest jet,"
Whom almost any lady'd
  Have given her eyes to get?

Does not her conscience smite her
  For one who hourly pines,
Thinking her bright eyes brighter
  Than any star that shines—
I mean of course the writer
  Of these pathetic lines?

Who knows? As quoth Sir Walter,
  "Time rolls his ceaseless course:
"The Grace of yore" may alter—
  And then, I've one resource:
I'll invest in a bran-new halter,
  And I'll perish without remorse.

LINES SUGGESTED BY THE FOURTEENTH
OF FEBRUARY.

ERE the morn the East has crimsoned,
　　When the stars are twinkling there,
(As they did in Watts's Hymns, and
　　Made him wonder what they were :)
When the forest-nymphs are beading
　　Fern and flower with silvery dew—
My infallible proceeding
　　Is to wake, and think of you.

When the hunter's ringing bugle
　　Sounds farewell to field and copse,
And I sit before my frugal
　　Meal of gravy-soup and chops:
When (as Gray remarks) "the moping
　　Owl doth to the moon complain,"

And the hour suggests eloping—
  Fly my thoughts to you again.

May my dreams be granted never?
  Must I aye endure affliction
Rarely realised, if ever,
  In our wildest works of fiction?
Madly Romeo loved his Juliet;
  Copperfield began to pine
When he hadn't been to school yet—
  But their loves were cold to mine.

Give me hope, the least, the dimmest,
  Ere I drain the poisoned cup:
Tell me I may tell the chymist
  Nor to make that arsenic up!
Else the heart must cease to throb in
  This my breast; and when, in tones
Hushed, men ask, "Who killed Cock Robin?"
  They'll be told, "Miss Clara J——s."

A, B, C.

A is an Angel of blushing eighteen:

B is the Ball where the Angel was seen:

C is her Chaperon, who cheated at cards:

D is the Deuxtemps, with Frank of the Guards:

E is her Eye, killing slowly but surely:

F is the Fan, whence it peeped so demurely:

G is the Glove of superlative kid:

H is the Hand which it spitefully hid:

I is the Ice which the fair one demanded:

J is the Juvenile, that dainty who handed:

K is the Kerchief, a rare work of art:

L is the Lace which composed the chief part:

M is the old Maid who watch'd the chits dance:

N is the Nose she turned up at each glance:

O is the Olga (just then in its prime):

P is the Partner who wouldn't keep time:

Q 's a Quadrille, put instead of the Lancers:

R the Remonstrances made by the dancers:

S is the Supper, where all went in pairs:

T is the Twaddle they talked on the stairs:

U is the Uncle who "thought we'd be goin':"

V is the Voice which his niece replied 'No' in:

W is the Waiter, who sat up till eight:

X is his Exit, not rigidly straight:

Y is a Yawning fit caused by the Ball:

Z stands for Zero, or nothing at all.

TO MRS. GOODCHILD.

THE night-wind's shriek is pitiless and hollow,
　　The boding bat flits by on sullen wing,
And I sit desolate, like that "one swallow"
　　Who found (with horror) that he'd not brought
　　　　spring :
Lonely he who erst with venturous thumb
Drew from its pie-y lair the solitary plum.

And to my gaze the phantoms of the Past,
　　The cherished fictions of my boyhood, rise:
I see Red Ridinghood observe, aghast,
　　The fixed expression of her grandam's eyes;
I hear the fiendish chattering and chuckling
Which those misguided fowls raised at the Ugly
　　　　Duckling.

The House that Jack built—and the Malt that lay

    Within the House—the Rat that ate the Malt—

The Cat, that in that sanguinary way

    Punished the poor thing for its venial fault—

The Worrier-Dog—the Cow with crumpled horn—

And then—ah yes! and then—the Maiden all forlorn!

O Mrs. Gurton—(may I call thee Gammer?)

    Thou more than mother to my infant mind!

I loved thee better than I loved my grammar—

    I used to wonder why the Mice were blind,

And who was gardener to Mistress Mary,

And what—I don't know still—was meant by

    "quite contrary."

"Tota contraria," an "*Arundo Cami*"

    Has phrased it—which is possibly explicit,

Ingenious certainly—but all the same I

    Still ask, when coming on the word, 'What is

    it?'

There were more things in Mrs. Gurton's eye,
Mayhap, than are dreamed of in our philosophy.

No doubt the Editor of 'Notes and Queries'
    Or 'Things not generally known' could tell
The word's real force—my only lurking fear is
    That the great Gammer "didna ken hersel":
(I've precedent, yet feel I owe apology
For passing in this way to Scottish phraseology).

Also, dear Madam, I must ask your pardon
    For making this unwarranted digression,
Starting (I think) from Mistress Mary's garden:—
    And beg to send, with every expression
Of personal esteem, a Book of Rhymes,
For Master G. to read at miscellaneous times.

There is a youth, who keeps a 'crumpled Horn,'
    (Living next me, upon the selfsame story,)
And ever, 'twixt the midnight and the morn,

He solaces his soul with Annie Laurie.

The tune is good; the habit p'raps romantic;

But tending, if pursued, to drive one's neighbours

frantic.

And now,—at this unprecedented hour,

When the young Dawn is "trampling out the

stars,"—

I hear that youth—with more than usual power

And pathos—struggling with the first few

bars.

And I do think the amateur cornopean

Should be put down by law—but that's perhaps

Utopian.

Who knows what "things unknown" I might

have "bodied

Forth," if not checked by that absurd Too-too·?

But don't I know that when my friend has

plodded

Through the first verse, the second will ensue?

Considering which, dear Madam, I will merely

Send the beforenamed book—and am yours most

sincerely.

ODE—'ON A DISTANT PROSPECT' OF MAKING A FORTUNE.

NOW the "rosy morn appearing"
  Floods with light the dazzled heaven;
And the schoolboy groans on hearing
  That eternal clock strike seven:—
Now the waggoner is driving
  Tow'rds the fields his clattering wain;
Now the blue-bottle, reviving,
  Buzzes down his native pane.

But to me the morn is hateful:
  Wearily I stretch my legs,
Dress, and settle to my plateful
  Of (perhaps inferior) eggs.
Yesterday Miss Crump, by message,
  Mentioned "rent," which "p'raps I'd pay;"

And I have a dismal presage
   That she'll call, herself, to-day.

Once, I breakfasted off rosewood,
   Smoked through silver-mounted pipes—
Then how my patrician nose would
   Turn up at the thought of "swipes!"
Ale,—occasionally claret,—
   Graced my luncheon then;—and now
I drink porter in a garret,
   To be paid for heaven knows how.

When the evening shades are deepened,
   And I doff my hat and gloves,
No sweet bird is there to "cheep and
   Twitter twenty million loves;"
No dark-ringleted canaries
   Sing to me of "hungry foam;"
No imaginary "Marys"
   Call fictitious "cattle home."

Araminta, sweetest, fairest!

   Solace once of every ill!

How I wonder if thou bearest

   Mivins in remembrance still!

If that Friday night is banished

   From a once retentive mind,

When the others somehow vanished,

   And we two were left behind:—

When in accents low, yet thrilling,

   I did all my love declare;

Mentioned that I'd not a shilling—

   Hinted that we need not care:

And complacently you listened

   To my somewhat long address,

And I thought the tear that glistened

   In the downdropt eye said Yes.

Once, a happy child, I carolled

   O'er green lawns the whole day through,

Not unpleasingly apparelled
  In a tightish suit of blue :—
What a change has now passed o'er me !
  Now with what dismay I see
Every rising morn before me !
  Goodness gracious patience me !

And I'll prowl, a moodier Lara,
  Thro' the world, as prowls the bat,
And habitually wear a
  Cypress wreath around my hat :
And when Death snuffs out the taper
  Of my Life, (as soon he must),
I'll send up to every paper,
  "Died, T. Mivins; of disgust."

ISABEL.

NOW o'er the landscape crowd the deepening
   shades,
   And the shut lily cradles not the bee;
The red deer couches in the forest glades,
   And faint the echoes of the slumberous sea:
   And ere I rest, one prayer I'll breathe for thee,
The sweet Egeria of my lonely dreams:
   Lady, forgive, that ever upon me
   Thoughts of thee linger, as the soft starbeams
Linger on Merlin's rock, or dark Sabrina's streams.

On gray Pilatus once we loved to stray,
   And watch far off the glimmering roselight break
O'er the dim mountain-peaks, ere yet one ray
   Pierced the deep bosom of the mist-clad lake.

Oh! who felt not new life within him wake,
And his pulse quicken, and his spirit burn—
  (Save one we wot of, whom the cold *did* make
Feel "shooting pains in every joint in turn,")
When first he saw the sun gild thy green shores,
      Lucerne?

And years have past, and I have gazed once more
  On blue lakes glistening amid mountains blue;
And all seemed sadder, lovelier than before—
  For all awakened memories of you.
  Oh! had I had you by my side, in lieu
Of that red matron, whom the flies would worry,
  (Flies in those parts unfortunately do,)
Who walked so slowly, talked in such a hurry,
And with such wild contempt for stops and Lindley
      Murray!

O Isabel, the brightest, heavenliest theme
  That ere drew dreamer on to poësy,

Since "Peggy's locks" made Burns neglect his
    team,
  And Stella's smile lured Johnson from his tea—
  I may not tell thee what thou art to me!
But ever dwells the soft voice in my ear,
  Whispering of what Time is, what Man might be,
  Would he but "do the duty that lies near,"
And cut clubs, cards, champagne, balls, billiard-
    rooms, and beer.

LINES SUGGESTED BY THE FOURTEENTH
OF FEBRUARY.

DARKNESS succeeds to twilight:
Through lattice and through skylight
The stars no doubt, if one looked out,
   Might be observed to shine:
   And sitting by the embers
   I elevate my members
On a stray chair, and then and there
   Commence a Valentine.

   Yea! by St. Valentinus,
   Emma shall not be minus
What all young ladies, whate'er their grade is
   Expect to-day no doubt:
   Emma the fair, the stately—
   Whom I beheld so lately,

Smiling beneath the snow-white wreath
 Which told that she was "out."

 Wherefore fly to her, swallow,
 And mention that I'd "follow,"
And "pipe and trill," et cetera, till
 I died, had I but wings:
 Say the North's "true and tender,"
 The South an old offender;
And hint in fact, with your well-known tact,
 All kinds of pretty things.

 Say I grow hourly thinner,
 Simply abhor my dinner—
Tho' I do try and absorb some viand
 Each day, for form's sake merely:
 And ask her, when all's ended,
 And I am found extended,
With vest blood-spotted and cut carotid,
 To think on Her's sincerely.

"HIC *VIR*, HIC EST."

OFTEN, when o'er tree and turret,
  Eve a dying radiance flings,
By that ancient pile I linger
  Known familiarly as " King's."
And the ghosts of days departed
  Rise, and in my burning breast
All the undergraduate wakens,
  And my spirit is at rest.

What, but a revolting fiction,
  Seems the actual result
Of the Census's enquiries
  Made upon the 15th ult.?
Still my soul is in its boyhood;
  Nor of year or changes recks,

Though my scalp is almost hairless,
    And my figure grows convex.

Backward moves the kindly dial;
    And I'm numbered once again
With those noblest of their species
    Called emphatically 'Men':
Loaf, as I have loafed aforetime,
    Through the streets, with tranquil mind,
And a long-backed fancy-mongrel
    Trailing casually behind:

Past the Senate-house I saunter,
    Whistling with an easy grace;
Past the cabbage-stalks that carpet
    Still the beefy market-place;
Poising evermore the eye-glass
    In the light sarcastic eye,
Lest, by chance, some breezy nursemaid
    Pass, without a tribute, by.

Once, an unassuming Freshman,
  Thro' these wilds I wandered on,
Seeing in each house a College,
  Under every cap a Don:
Each perambulating infant
  Had a magic in its squall,
For my eager eye detected
  Senior Wranglers in them all.

By degrees my education
  Grew, and I became as others;
Learned to blunt my moral feelings
  By the aid of Bacon Brothers;
Bought me tiny boots of Mortlock,
  And colossal prints of Roe;
And ignored the proposition
  That both time and money go.

Learned to work the wary dogcart
  Artfully thro' King's Parade;

Dress, and steer a boat, and sport with
  Amaryllis in the shade:
Struck, at Brown's, the dashing hazard;
  Or (more curious sport than that)
Dropped, at Callaby's, the terrier
  Down upon the prisoned rat.

I have stood serene on Fenner's
  Ground, indifferent to blisters,
While the Buttress of the period
  Bowled me his peculiar twisters:
Sung 'We won't go home till morning';
  Striven to part my backhair straight;
Drunk (not lavishly) of Miller's
  Old dry wines at 78/:—

When within my veins the blood ran,
  And the curls were on my brow,
I did, oh ye undergraduates,
 'Much as ye are doing now.

Wherefore bless ye, O beloved ones:—

Now unto mine inn must I,

Your 'poor moralist,'* betake me,

In my 'solitary fly.'

---

* "Poor moralist, and what art thou?
  A solitary fly."

        GRAY.

BEER.

IN those old days which poets say were golden—
 (Perhaps they laid the gilding on themselves :
And, if they did, I'm all the more beholden
  To those brown dwellers in my dusty shelves,
Who talk to me "in language quaint and olden"
  Of gods and demigods and fauns and elves,
Pan with his pipes, and Bacchus with his leopards,
And staid young goddesses who flirt with shepherds :)

In those old days, the Nymph called Etiquette
 (Appalling thought to dwell on) was not born.
They had their May, but no Mayfair as yet,
  No fashions varying as the hues of morn.

Just as they pleased they dressed and drank and ate,

  Sang hymns to Ceres (their John Barleycorn)

And danced unchaperoned, and laughed unchecked,

And were no doubt extremely incorrect.

Yet do I think their theory was pleasant:

  And oft, I own, my ' wayward fancy roams '

Back to those times, so different from the present;

  When no one smoked cigars, nor gave At-homes,

Nor smote a billiard-ball, nor winged a pheasant,

  Nor ' did' her hair by means of long-tailed combs,

Nor migrated to Brighton once a year,

Nor—most astonishing of all—drank Beer.

No, they did not drink Beer, " which brings me to "

  (As Gilpin said) "the middle of my song."

Not that "the middle " is precisely true,

  Or else I should not tax your patience long:

If I had said ' beginning,' it might do;

  But I have a dislike to quoting wrong:

I was unlucky—sinned against, not sinning—
When Cowper wrote down 'middle' for 'beginning.'

So to proceed. That abstinence from Malt
 Has always struck me as extremely curious.
The Greek mind must have had some vital fault,
 That they should stick to liquors so injurious—
(Wine, water, tempered p'raps with Attic salt)—
 And not at once invent that mild, luxurious,
And artful beverage, Beer. How the digestion
Got on without it, is a startling question.

Had they digestions? and an actual body
 Such as dyspepsia might make attacks on?
Were they abstract ideas—(like Tom Noddy
 And Mr. Briggs)—or men, like Jones and Jackson?
Then nectar—was that beer, or whisky-toddy?
 Some say the Gaelic mixture, *I* the Saxon:
I think a strict adherence to the latter
Might make some Scots less pigheaded, and fatter.

E

Besides, Bon Gaultier definitely shews

That the real beverage for feasting gods on

Is a soft compound, grateful to the nose

And also to the palate, known as 'Hodgson.'

I know a man—a tailor's son—who rose

To be a peer: and this I would lay odds on,

(Though in his Memoirs it may not appear,)

That that man owed his rise to copious Beer.

O Beer! O Hodgson, Guinness, Allsop, Bass!

Names that should be on every infant's tongue!

Shall days and months and years and centuries
  pass,

And still your merits be unrecked, unsung?

Oh! I have gazed into my foaming glass,

And wished that lyre could yet again be strung

Which once rang prophet-like through Greece, and
  taught her

Misguided sons that the best drink was water.

How would he now recant that wild opinion,
  And sing—as would that I could sing—of you!
I was not born (alas!) the "Muses' minion,"
  I'm not poetical, not even blue:
And he, we know, but strives with waxen pinion,
  Whoe'er he is that entertains the view
Of emulating Pindar, and will be
Sponsor at last to some now nameless sea.

Oh! when the green slopes of Arcadia burned
  With all the lustre of the dying day,
And on Cithæron's brow the reaper turned,
  (Humming, of course, in his delightful way,
How Lycidas was dead, and how concerned
  The Nymphs were when they saw his lifeless clay;
And how rock told to rock the dreadful story
That poor young Lycidas was gone to glory:)

What would that lone and labouring soul have given,
  At that soft moment for a pewter pot!

How had the mists that dimmed his eye been riven,
  And Lycidas and sorrow all forgot!
If his own grandmother had died unshriven,
  In two short seconds he'd have recked it not;
Such power hath Beer.   The heart which Grief hath
    canker'd
Hath one unfailing remedy—the Tankard.

Coffee is good, and so no doubt is cocoa;
  Tea did for Johnson and the Chinamen:
When 'Dulce est desipere in loco'
  Was written, real Falernian winged the pen.
When a rapt audience has encored 'Fra Poco'
  Or 'Casta Diva,' I have heard that then
The Prima Donna, smiling herself out,
Recruits her flagging powers with bottled stout.

But what is coffee, but a noxious berry,
  Born to keep used-up Londoners awake?

What is Falernian, what is Port or Sherry,

    But vile concoctions to make dull heads ache?

Nay stout itself—(though good with oysters, very)—

    Is not a thing your reading man should take.

He that would shine, and petrify his tutor,

Should drink draught Allsop in its " native pewter."

But hark! a sound is stealing on my ear—

    A soft and silvery sound—I know it well.

Its tinkling tells me that a time is near

    Precious to me—it is the Dinner Bell.

O blessed Bell! Thou bringest beef and beer,

    Thou bringest good things more than tongue may

        tell:

Seared is, of course, my heart—but unsubdued

Is, and shall be, my appetite for food.

I go. Untaught and feeble is my pen:

    But on one statement I may safely venture:

That few of our most highly gifted men

    Have more appreciation of the trencher.

I go. One pound of British beef, and then

    What Mr. Swiveller called a " modest quencher";

That home-returning, I may ' soothly say,'

" Fate cannot touch me : I have dined to-day."

ODE TO TOBACCO.

THOU who, when fears attack,
Bidst them avaunt, and Black
Care, at the horseman's back

    Perching, unseatest;
Sweet when the morn is gray;
Sweet, when they've cleared away
Lunch; and at close of day

    Possibly sweetest:

I have a liking old
For thee, though manifold
Stories; I know, are told,

    Not to thy credit;

How one (or two at most)
Drops make a cat a ghost—
Useless, except to roast—
    Doctors have said it:

How they who use fusees
All grow by slow degrees
Brainless as chimpanzees,
    Meagre as lizards ;
Go mad, and beat their. wives ;
Plunge (after shocking lives)
Razors and carving knives
    Into their gizzards.

Confound such knavish tricks !
Yet know I five or six
Smokers who freely mix
    Still with their neighbours ;
Jones—who, I'm glad to say,

Asked leave of Mrs. J.)—

Daily absorbs a clay

    After his labours.

Cats may have had their goose

Cooked by tobacco-juice;

Still why deny its use

    Thoughtfully taken?

We're not as tabbies are:

Smith, take a fresh cigar!

Jones, the tobacco-jar!

    Here's to thee, Bacon!

DOVER TO MUNICH.

FAREWELL, farewell! Before our prow
  Leaps in white foam the noisy channel;
A tourist's cap is on my brow,
  My legs are cased in tourist's flannel:

Around me gasp the invalids—
  The quantity to-night is fearful—
I take a brace or so of weeds,
  And feel (as yet) extremely cheerful.

The night wears on:—my thirst I quench
  With one imperial pint of porter;
Then drop upon a casual bench—
  (The bench is short, but I am shorter)—

Place 'neath my head the *havre-sac*
　Which I have stowed my little all in,
And sleep, though moist about the back,
　Serenely in an old tarpaulin.

———

Bed at Ostend at 5 A.M.
　Breakfast at 6, and train 6.30,
Tickets to Königswinter (mem.
　The seats unutterably dirty).

And onward thro' those dreary flats
　We move, with scanty space to sit on,
Flanked by stout girls with steeple hats,
　And waists that paralyse a Briton ;—

By many a tidy little town,
　Where tidy little Fraus sits knitting;
(The men's pursuits are, lying down,
　Smoking perennial pipes, and spitting;)

And doze, and execrate the heat,
 And wonder how far off Cologne is,
And if we shall get aught to eat,
 Till we get there, save raw polonies:

Until at last the "gray old pile"
 Is seen, is past, and three hours later
We're ordering steaks, and talking vile
 Mock-German to an Austrian waiter.

———

Königswinter, hateful Königswinter!
 Burying-place of all I loved so well!
Never did the most extensive printer
 Print a tale so dark as thou couldst tell!

In the sapphire West the eve yet lingered,
 Bathed in kindly light those hill-tops cold;
Fringed each cloud, and, stooping rosy-fingered,
 Changed Rhine's waters into molten gold;—

'hile still nearer did his light waves splinter
   Into silvery shafts the streaming light;
And I said I loved thee, Königswinter,
   For the glory that was thine that night.

And we gazed, till slowly disappearing,
   Like a day-dream, passed the pageant by,
And I saw but those lone hills, uprearing
   Dull dark shapes against a hueless sky.

Then I turned, and on those bright hopes pondered
   Whereof yon gay fancies were the type;
And my hand mechanically wandered
   Towards my left-hand pocket for a pipe.

Ah! why starts each eyeball from its socket,
   As, in Hamlet, start the guilty Queen's?
There, deep-hid in its accustomed pocket,
   Lay my sole pipe, smashed to smithereens!

On, on the vessel steals;
Round go the paddle-wheels,
And now the tourist feels
 As he should;
For king-like rolls the Rhine,
And the scenery's divine,
And the victuals and the wine
 Rather good.

From every crag we pass 'll
Rise up some hoar old castle;
The hanging fir-groves tassel
 Every slope;
And the vine her lithe arms stretches
Over peasants singing catches—
And you'll make no end of sketches,
 I should hope.

We 've a nun here (called Therèse),

Two couriers out of place,

One Yankee with a face

    Like a ferret's :

And three youths in scarlet caps

Drinking chocolate and schnapps—

A diet which perhaps

    Has its merits.

And day again declines :

In shadow sleep the vines,

And the last ray thro' the pines

    Feebly glows,

Then sinks behind yon ridge ;

And the usual evening midge

Is settling on the bridge

    Of my nose.

And keen's the air and cold,

And the sheep are in the fold,

And Night walks sable-stoled

    Thro' the trees;

And on the silent river

The floating starbeams quiver;—

And now, the saints deliver

    Us from fleas.

———

Avenues of broad white houses,

    Basking in the noontide glare;—

Streets, which foot of traveller shrinks from,

    As on hot plates shrinks the bear;—

Elsewhere lawns, and vista'd gardens,

    Statues white, and cool arcades,

Where at eve the German warrior

    Winks upon the German maids;—

Such is Munich:—broad and stately,
   Rich of hue, and fair of form;
But, towards the end of August,
   Unequivocally *warm*.

There, the long dim galleries threading,
   May· the artist's eye behold
Breathing from the "deathless canvass"
   Records of the years of old:

Pallas there, and Jove, and Juno,
   "Take" once more their "walks abroad,"
Under Titian's fiery woodlands
   And the saffron skies of Claude:

        •

There the Amazons of Rubens
   Lift the failing arm to strike,
And the pale light falls in masses
   On the horsemen of Vandyke;

F

And in Berghem's pools reflected
  Hang the cattle's graceful shapes,
And Murillo's soft boy-faces
  Laugh amid the Seville grapes;

And all purest, loveliest fancies
  That in poets' souls may dwell
Started into shape and substance
  At the touch of Raphael.

Lo! her wan arms folded meekly,
  And the glory of her hair
Falling as a robe around her,
  Kneels the Magdalen in prayer;

And the white-robed Virgin-mother
  Smiles, as centuries back she smiled,
Half in gladness, half in wonder,
  On the calm face of her Child:—

And that mighty Judgment-vision
    Tells how man essayed to climb
Up the ladder of the ages,
    Past the frontier-walls of Time;

Heard the trumpet-echoes rolling
    Thro' the phantom-peopled sky,
And the still voice bid this mortal
    Put on immortality.

      *   *   *   *

Thence we turned, what time the blackbird
    Pipes to vespers from his perch,
And from out the clattering city
    Pass'd into the silent church;

Mark'd the shower of sunlight breaking
    Thro' the crimson panes o'erhead,
And on pictured wall and window
    Read the histories of the dead:

Till the kneelers round us, rising,

   Crossed their foreheads and were gone;

And o'er aisle and arch and cornice,

   Layer on layer, the night came on.

CHARADES.

I.

SHE stood at Greenwich, motionless amid
  The ever-shifting crowd of passengers.
I mark'd a big tear quivering on the lid
  Of her deep-lustrous eye, and knew that hers
  Were days of bitterness.   But, "Oh! what stirs"
I said "such storm within so fair a breast?"
  Even as I spoke, two apoplectic curs
Came feebly up: with one wild cry she prest
Each singly to her heart, and faltered, "Heaven
      be blest!"

Yet once again I saw her, from the deck
  Of a black ship that steamed towards Blackwall.

She walked upon *my first*. Her stately neck

   Bent o'er an object shrouded in her shawl:

I could not see the tears—the glad tears—fall,

Yet knew they fell. And "Ah," I said, "not puppies,

      puppies,

   Seen unexpectedly, could lift the pall

From hearts who *know* what tasting misery's cup is

As Niobe's, or mine, or blighted William Guppy's."

————

Spake John Grogblossom the coachman to Eliza

   Spinks the cook:

"Mrs. Spinks," says he, "I've founder'd: 'Liza

   dear, I'm overtook.

Druv into a corner reglar, puzzled as a babe unborn;

Speak the word, my blessed 'Liza; speak, and John

   the coachman's yourn."

Then Eliza Spinks made answer, blushing, to the

   coachman John:

ohn, I'm born and bred a spinster: I've begun
   and I'll go on.

dless cares and endless worrits, well I knows it,
   has a wife:

)king for a genteel family, John, it's a goluptious
   life!

gets £20 per annum—tea and things o' course
   not reckoned,—

ere's a cat that eats the butter, takes the coals,
   and breaks *my second*:

ere's soci'ty—James the footman;—(not that I
   look after him;

t he's aff'ble in his manners, with amazing
   length of limb;)—

Tever durst the missis enter here until I've said
   ' Come in':

I saw the master peeping, I'd catch up the
   rolling-pin.

Christmas-boxes, that's a something; perkisites,
 that's something too;
And I think, take all together, John, I won't be on
 with you."

John the coachman took his hat up, for he thought
 he'd had enough;
Rubb'd an elongated forehead with a meditative
 cuff;
Paused before the stable doorway; said, when there,
 in accents mild,
"She's a fine young 'oman, cook is; but that's
 where it is, she's spiled."

———

I have read in some not marvellous tale,
 (Or if I have not, I've dreamed)
Of one who filled up the convivial cup
 Till the company round him seemed

To be vanished and gone, tho' the lamps upon
  Their face as aforetime gleamed:
And his head sunk down, and a Lethe crept
O'er his powerful brain, and the young man slept.

Then they laid him with care in his moonlit bed:
  But first—having thoughtfully fetched some tar—
Adorn'd him with feathers, aware that the weather's
  Uncertainty brings on at nights catarrh.

They staid in his room till the sun was high:
  But still did the feathered one give no sign
Of opening a peeper—he might be a sleeper
  Such as rests on the Northern or Midland line.

  At last he woke, and with profound
  Bewilderment he gazed around;
  Dropped one, then both feet to the ground,
  But never spake a word:

Then to *my whole* he made his way;

Took one long lingering survey;

And softly, as he stole away,

Remarked, "By Jove, a bird!"

II.

IF you 've seen a short man swagger tow'rds the
    footlights at Shoreditch,
Sing out "Heave aho! my hearties," and perpetually
    hitch
Up, by an ingenious movement, trousers innocent
    of brace,
Briskly flourishing a cudgel in his pleased com-
    panion's face;

If he preluded with hornpipes each successive thing
    he did,
From a sun-browned cheek extracting still an os-
    tentatious quid;
And expectorated freely, and occasionally cursed :—

Then have you beheld, depicted by a master's hand,
 my first.

O my countryman! if ever from thy arm the bolster
 sped,
In thy school-days, with precision at a young com-
 panion's head;
If 'twas thine to lodge the marble in the centre of
 the ring,
Or with well-directed pebble make the sitting hen
 take wing:

Then do thou—each fair May morning, when the
 blue lake is as glass,
And the gossamers are twinkling star-like in the
 beaded grass;
When the mountain-bee is sipping fragrance from
 the bluebell's lip,
And the bathing-woman tells you, Now's your time
 to take a dip:

When along the misty valleys fieldward winds the
    lowing herd,

And the early worm is being dropped on by the
    early bird;

And Aurora hangs her jewels from the bending
    rose's cup,

And the myriad voice of Nature calls thee to *my*
    second up :—

Hie thee to the breezy common, where the melan-
    choly goose

Stalks, and the astonished donkey finds that he is
    really loose;

There amid green fern and furze-bush shalt thou
    soon *my whole* behold,

Rising 'bull-eyed and majestic'—as Olympus' queen
    of old:

Kneel,—at a respectful distance,—as they kneeled
    to her, and try

With judicious hand to put a ball into that ball-less

eye :

Till a stiffness seize thy elbows, and the general

public wake—

Then return, and, clear of conscience, walk into thy

well-earned steak.

III.

ERE yet "knowledge for the million"
  Came out "neatly bound in boards";
When like Care upon a pillion
  Matrons rode behind their lords:
Rarely, save to hear the Rector,
  Forth did younger ladies roam;
Making pies, and brewing nectar
  From the gooseberry-trees at home.

They'd not dreamed of Pau or Vevay;
  Ne'er should into blossom burst
At the ball or at the levée;
  Never come, in fact, *my first:*
Nor illumine cards by dozens
  With some labyrinthine text,
Nor work smoking-caps for cousins
  Who were pounding at *my next.*

Now have skirts, and minds, grown ampler;
  Now not all they seek to do
Is create upon a sampler
  Beasts which Buffon never knew:
But their venturous muslins rustle
  O'er the cragstone and the snow,
Or at home their biceps muscle
  Grows by practising the bow.

Worthy they those dames who, fable
  Says, rode "palfreys" to the war
With some giant Thane, whose "sable
  Destrier caracoled" before;
Smiled, as—springing from the war-horse
  As men spring in modern 'cirques'—
He plunged, ponderous as a four-horse
  Coach, among the vanished Turks:—

In the good times when the jester
  Asked the monarch how he was,

And the landlady addrest her
  Guests as 'gossip' or as 'coz';
When the Templar said, "Gramercy,"
  Or, "'Twas shrewdly thrust, i' fegs,"
To Sir Halbert or Sir Percy
  As they knocked him off his legs:

And, by way of mild reminders
  That he needed coin, the Knight
Day by day extracted grinders
  From the howling Israelite:
And *my whole* in merry Sherwood
  Sent, with preterhuman luck,
Missiles—not of steel but firwood—
  Thro' the two-mile-distant buck.

IV.

EVENING threw soberer hue

Over the blue sky, and the few

Poplars that grew just in the view

Of the hall of Sir Hugo de Wynkle:

"Answer me true," pleaded Sir Hugh,

(Striving some hardhearted maiden to woo,)

"What shall I do, Lady, for you?

'Twill be done, ere your eye may twinkle.

Shall I borrow the wand of a Moorish enchanter,

And bid a decanter contain the Levant, or

The brass from the face of a Mormonite ranter?

Shall I go for the mule of the Spanish Infantar—

(That *r*, for the sake of the line, we must grant

her,)—

And race with the foul fiend, and beat in a canter,

Like that first of equestrians Tam o' Shanter?

I talk not mere banter—say not that I can't, or

By this *my first*—(a Virginia planter

Sold it me to kill rats)—I will die instanter."

    The Lady bended her ivory neck, and

    Whispered mournfully, "Go for—*my second.*"

    She said, and the red from Sir Hugh's cheek

        fled,

    And "Nay," did he say, as he stalked away

      The fiercest of injured men:

    "Twice have I humbled my haughty soul,

    And on bended knee have I pressed *my whole*—

      But I never will press it again!"

V.

ON pinnacled St. Mary's
  Lingers the setting sun;
Into the streets the blackguards
  Are skulking one by one:
Butcher and Boots and Bargeman
  Lay pipe and pewter down;
And with wild shout come tumbling out
  To join the Town and Gown.

And now the undergraduates
  Come forth by twos and threes,
From the broad tower of Trinity,
  From the green gate of Caius:
The wily bargeman marks them,
  And swears to do his worst;
To turn to impotence their strength,
  And their beauty to *my first*.

But before Corpus gateway

　My second first arose,

When Barnacles the Freshman

　Was pinned upon the nose:

Pinned on the nose by Boxer,

　Who brought a hobnailed herd

From Barnwell, where he kept a van,

Being indeed a dogsmeat man,

Vendor of terriers, blue or tan,

　And dealer in *my third.*

'Twere long to tell how Boxer

　Was 'countered' on the cheek,

And knocked into the middle

　Of the ensuing week:

How Barnacles the Freshman

　Was asked his name and college;

And how he did the fatal facts

　Reluctantly acknowledge.

He called upon the Proctor

    Next day at half-past ten;

Men whispered that the Freshman cut

    A different figure then:—

That the brass forsook his forehead,

    The iron fled his soul,

As with blanched lip and visage wan

Before the stony-hearted Don

    He kneeled upon *my whole*.

VI.

SIKES, housebreaker, of Houndsditch,
 Habitually swore;
But so surpassingly profane
 He never was before,
As on a night in winter,
 When—softly as he stole
In the dim light from stair to stair,
Noiseless as boys who in her lair
Seek to surprise a fat old hare—
He barked his shinbone, unaware
 Encountering *my whole*.

As pours the Anio plainward,
 When rains have swollen the dykes,
So, with such noise, poured down *my first*
 Stirred by the shins of Sikes.

The Butler Bibulus heard it;
   And straightway ceased to snore,
And sat up, like an egg on end,
   While men might count a score:
Then spake he to Tigerius,
   A Buttons bold was he:
"Buttons, I think there's thieves about;
Just strike a light and tumble out;
If you can't find one go without,
   And see what you may see."

But now was all the household,
   Almost, upon its legs,
Each treading carefully about
   As if they trod on eggs.
With robe far-streaming issued
   Paterfamilias forth;
And close behind him,—stout and true
   And tender as the North,—

Came Mrs. P., supporting

    On her broad arm her fourth.

Betsy the nurse, who never

    From largest beetle ran,

And—conscious p'raps of pleasing caps—

    The housemaids, formed the van:

And Bibulus the butler,

    His calm brows slightly arched;

(No mortal wight had ere that night

    Seen him with shirt unstarched;)

And Bob the shockhaired knifeboy,

    Wielding two Sheffield blades,

And James Plush of the sinewy legs,

    The love of lady's maids:

And charwoman and chaplain

    Stood mingled in a mass,

And "Things," thought he of Houndsditch,

    "Is come to a pretty pass."

Beyond all things a baby
  Is to the schoolgirl dear;
Next to herself the nursemaid loves
  Her dashing grenadier;
Only with life the sailor
  Parts from the British flag;
While one hope lingers, the cracksman's fingers
  Drop not his hard-earned swag.

But, as hares do *my second*
  Thro' green Calabria's copses,
As females vanish at the sight
  Of short-horns and of wopses;
So, dropping forks and teaspoons,
  The pride of Houndsditch fled,
Dumbfoundered by the hue and cry
  He'd raised up overhead.

* * * * *

They gave him—did the judges—

    As much as was his due.

And, Saxon, shouldst thou e'er be led

    To deem this tale untrue;

Then—any night in winter,

    When the cold north wind blows,

And bairns are told to keep out cold

    By tallowing the nose:

When round the fire the elders

    Are gathered in a bunch,

And the girls are doing crochet,

    And the boys are reading Punch:—

Go thou and look in Leech's book;

    There haply shalt thou spy

A stout man on a staircase stand,

With aspect anything but bland,

And rub his right shin with his hand,

    To witness if I lie.

PROVERBIAL PHILOSOPHY.

Introductory.

ART thou beautiful, O my daughter, as the
    budding rose of April?

Are all thy motions music, and is poetry throned
    in thine eye?

Then hearken unto me; and I will make the bud
    a fair flower,

I will plant it upon the bank of Elegance, and
    water it with the water of Cologne;

And in the season it shall "come out," yea bloom,
    the pride of the parterre;

Ladies shall marvel at its beauty, and a Lord shall
    pluck it at the last.

Of Propriety.

Study first Propriety: for she is indeed the Pole-
    star

Which shall guide the artless maiden through the
    mazes of Vanity Fair;

Nay, she is the golden chain which holdeth to-
    gether Society;

The lamp by whose light young Psyche shall ap-
    proach unblamed her Eros.

Verily Truth is as Eve, which was ashamed being
    naked;

Wherefore doth Propriety dress her with the fair
    foliage of artifice:

And when she is drest, behold! she knoweth not
    herself again.—

I walked in the Forest; and above me stood the
    Yew,

Stood like a slumbering giant, shrouded in im-
penetrable shade;

Then I pass'd into the citizen's garden, and marked
a tree clipt into shape,

(The giant's locks had been shorn by the Dalilah-
shears of Decorum;)

And I said, "Surely nature is goodly; but how
much goodlier is Art!"

I heard the wild notes of the lark floating far over
the blue sky,

And my foolish heart went after him, and, lo!
I blessed him as he rose;

Foolish! for far better is the trained boudoir
bulfinch,

Which pipeth the semblance of a tune, and mechanically draweth up water:

And the reinless steed of the desert, though his
neck be clothed with thunder,

Must yield to him that danceth and 'moveth in the
circles' at Astley's.

For verily, O my daughter, the world is a masque-
rade,

And God made thee one thing, that thou mightest
make thyself another:

A maiden's heart is as champagne, ever aspiring
and struggling upwards,

And it needed that its motions be checked by the
silvered cork of Propriety:

He that can afford the price, his be the precious
treasure,

Let him drink deeply of its sweetness, nor grumble
if it tasteth of the cork.

Of Friendship.

Choose judiciously thy friends; for to discard them
is undesirable,

Yet it is better to drop thy friends, O my daughter, than to drop thy 'H's'.

Dost thou know a wise woman? yea, wiser than the children of light?

Hath she a position? and a title? and are her parties in the Morning Post?

If thou dost, cleave unto her, and give up unto her thy body and mind;

Think with her ideas, and distribute thy smiles at her bidding:

So shalt thou become like unto her; and thy manners shall be "formed,"

And thy name shall be a Sesame, at which the doors of the great shall fly open:

Thou shalt know every Peer, his arms, and the date of his creation,

His pedigree and their intermarriages, and cousins to the sixth remove:

Thou shalt kiss the hand of Royalty, and lo! in
next morning's papers,

Side by side with rumours of wars, and stories of
shipwrecks and sieges,

Shall appear thy name, and the minutiæ of thy
head-dress and petticoat,

For an enraptured public to muse upon over their
matutinal muffin.

Of Reading.

Read not Milton, for he is dry; nor Shakespeare,
for he wrote of common life:

Nor Scott, for his romances, though fascinating,
are yet intelligible:

Nor Thackeray, for he is a Hogarth, a photographer
who flattereth not:

Nor Kingsley, for he shall teach thee that thou
shouldest not dream, but do.

H

Read incessantly thy Burke; that Burke who, nobler
    than he of old,

Treateth of the Peer and Peeress, the truly Sublime
    and Beautiful:

Likewise study the " creations" of " the Prince of
    modern Romance ";

Sigh over Leonard the Martyr, and smile on
    Pelham the puppy:

Learn how " love is the dram-drinking of ex-
    istence ";

And how we " invoke, in the Gadara of our still
    closets,

The beautiful ghost of the Ideal, with the simple
    wand of the pen."

Listen how Maltravers and the orphan " forgot all
    but love,"

And how Devereux's family chaplain " made and
    unmade kings ":

How Eugene Aram, though a thief, a liar, and
    a murderer,

Yet, being intellectual, was amongst the noblest of
mankind.

So shalt thou live in a world peopled with heroes
and master-spirits;

And if thou canst not realize the Ideal, thou shalt
at least idealize the Real.

TRANSLATIONS.

LYCIDAS.

YET once more, O ye laurels! and once more,
Ye myrtles brown, with ivy never sere,
I come to pluck your berries harsh and crude,
And with forced fingers rude
Shatter your leaves before the mellowing year.
Bitter constraint, and sad occasion dear,
Compels me to disturb your season due;
For Lycidas is dead, dead ere his prime,
Young Lycidas, and hath not left his peer:
Who would not sing for Lycidas? He knew
Himself to sing, and build the lofty rhyme.
He must not float upon his watery bier
Unwept, and welter to the parching wind,
Without the meed of some melodious tear.

LYCIDAS.

EN! iterum laurus, iterum salvete myricæ
Pallentes, nullique hederæ quæ ceditis ævo.
Has venio baccas, quanquam sapor asper acerbis,
Decerptum, quassumque manu folia ipsa proterva,
Maturescentem prævortens improbus annum.
Causa gravis, pia causa, subest, et amara deûm lex;
Nec jam sponte mea vobis rata tempora turbo.
Nam periit Lycidas, periit superante juventa
Imberbis Lycidas, nec par manet illius alter.
Quis cantare super Lycida neget? Ipse quoque artem
Nôrat Apollineam, versumque imponere versu.
Non nullo vitreum fas innatet ille feretrum
Flente, voluteturque arentes corpus ad auras,
Indotatum adeo et lacrymæ vocalis egenum.

Begin then, sisters of the sacred well,

That from beneath the seat of Jove doth spring;

Begin, and somewhat loudly sweep the string.

Hence with denial vain, and coy excuse,

So may some gentle muse

With lucky words favour my destined urn,

And, as he passes, turn

And bid fair peace be to my sable shroud:

· For we were nursed upon the self-same hill,

Fed the same flock by fountain, shade, and rill.

Together both, ere the high lawns appeared

Under the opening eyelids of the morn,

We drove afield, and both together heard

What time the gray fly winds her sultry horn,

Battening our flocks with the fresh dews of night,

Oft till the star that rose, at evening, bright,

Toward Heaven's descent had sloped his westering

wheel.

Quare agite, o sacri fontis queis cura, sorores,

Cui sub inaccessi sella Jovis exit origo:

Incipite, et sonitu graviore impellite chordas.

Lingua procul male prompta loqui, suasorque mo-
  rarum

Sit pudor: alloquiis ut mollior una secundis

Pieridum faveat, cui mox ego destiner, urnæ:

Et gressus prætergrediens convertat, et "Esto"

Dicat "amœna quies atra tibi veste latenti:"

Uno namque jugo duo nutribamur: easdem

Pascebamus oves ad fontem et rivulum et um-
  bram.

Tempore nos illo, nemorum convexa priusquam,

Aurora reserante oculos, cœpere videri,

Urgebamus equos ad pascua: novimus horam

Aridus audiri solitus qua clangor asili;

Rore recente greges passi pinguescere noctis

Sæpius, albuerat donec quod vespere sidus

Hesperios axes prono inclinasset Olympo.

Meanwhile the rural ditties were not mute,
Tempered to the oaten flute;
Rough satyrs danced, and fauns with cloven heel
From the glad sound would not be absent long,
And old Damætas loved to hear our song.

But oh, the heavy change, now thou art gone,
Now thou art gone, and never must return!
Thee, shepherd, thee the woods, and desert caves
With wild thyme and the gadding vine o'ergrown,
And all their echoes mourn.
The willows, and the hazel copses green,
Shall now no more be seen,
Fanning their joyous leaves to thy soft lays.
As killing as the canker to the rose,
Or taint-worm to the weanling herds that graze,
Or frost to flowers, that their gay wardrobe wear,
When first the white-thorn blows;
Such, Lycidas, thy loss to shepherd's ear.

Where were ye, nymphs, when the remorseless deep

At pastorales non cessavere camœnæ,

Fistula disparibus quas temperat apta cicutis:

Saltabant Satyri informes, nec murmure læto

Capripedes potuere diu se avertere Fauni;

Damætasque modos nostros longævus amabat.

    Jamque, relicta tibi, quantum mutata viden-

       tur

Rura—relicta tibi, cui non spes ulla regressûs!

Te sylvæ, teque antra, puer, deserta ferarum,

Incultis obducta thymis ac vite sequaci,

Decessisse gemunt; gemitusque reverberat Echo.

Non salices, non glauca ergo coryleta videbo

Molles ad numeros lætum motare cacumen:—

Quale rosis scabies; quam formidabile vermis

Depulso jam lacte gregi, dum tondet agellos;

Sive quod, indutis verna jam veste, pruinæ

Floribus, albet ubi primum paliurus in agris:

Tale fuit nostris, Lycidam periise, bubulcis.

    Qua, Nymphæ, latuistis, ubi crudele profundum

Closed o'er the head of your loved Lycidas?

For neither were ye playing on the steep,

Where your old bards, the famous Druids, lie;

Nor on the shaggy top of Mona high,

Nor yet where Deva spreads her wizard stream:

Ay me! I fondly dream!

Had ye been there, for what could that have done?

What could the muse herself that Orpheus bore,

The muse herself for her enchanting son,

Whom universal nature did lament,

When by the rout that made the hideous roar,

His gory visage down the stream was sent,

Down the swift Hebrus to the Lesbian shore?

   Alas! what boots it with incessant care

To tend the homely slighted shepherd's trade,

And strictly meditate the thankless muse?

Were it not better done as others use,

To sport with Amaryllis in the shade,

Or with the tangles of Neæra's hair?

Delicias Lycidam vestras sub vortice torsit?

Nam neque vos scopulis tum ludebatis in illis

Quos veteres, Druidæ, vates, illustria servant

Nomina; nec celsæ setoso in culmine Monæ,

Nec, quos Deva locos magicis amplectitur undis.

Væ mihi! delusos exercent somnia sensus:

Venissetis enim; numquid venisse juvaret?

Numquid Pieris ipsa parens interfuit Orphei,

Pieris ipsa suæ sobolis, qui carmine rexit

Corda virum, quem terra olim, quam magna, dolebat,

Tempore quo, dirum auditu strepitante caterva,

Ora secundo amni missa, ac fœdata cruore,

Lesbia præcipitans ad litora detulit Hebrus?

Eheu quid prodest noctes instare diesque

Pastorum curas spretas humilesque tuendo,

Nilque relaturam meditari rite Camœnam?

Nonne fuit satius lusus agitare sub umbra,

(Ut mos est aliis,) Amaryllida sive Neæram

Sectanti, ac tortis digitum impediisse capillis?

Fame is the spur that the clear spirit doth raise

(That last infirmity of noble mind)

To scorn delights, and live laborious days.

But the fair guerdon when we hope to find,

And think to burst out into sudden blaze,

Comes the blind fury with the abhorred shears,

And slits the thin-spun life.   "But not the praise,"

Phœbus replied, and touched my trembling ears;

"Fame is no plant that grows on mortal soil,

Nor in the glistering foil

Set off to the world, nor in broad rumour lies,

But lives and spreads aloft by those pure eyes,

And perfect witness of all-judging Jove;

As he pronounces lastly on each deed,

Of so much fame in Heaven expect thy meed."

O fountain Arethuse, and thou honoured flood,

Smooth-sliding Mincius, crowned with vocal reeds,

That strain I heard was of a higher mood:

Scilicet ingenuum cor Fama, novissimus error

Illa animi majoris, uti calcaribus urget

Spernere delicias ac dedi rebus agendis.

Quanquam—exoptatam jam spes attingere dotem;

Jam nec opinata remur splendescere flamma:—

Cæca sed invisa cum forfice venit Erinnys,

Hærentemque secat tenui subtemine vitam.

"At Famam non illa," refert, tangitque trementes

Phœbus Apollo aures.   "Fama haud, vulgaris ad
      instar

Floris, amat terrestre solum, fictosque nitores

Queis inhiat populus, nec cum Rumore patescit.

Vivere dant illi, dant increbrescere late

Puri oculi ac vox summa Jovis, cui sola Potestas.

Fecerit ille semel de facto quoque virorum

Arbitrium : tantum famæ manet æthera nactis."

Fons Arethusa! sacro placidus qui laberis alveo,

Frontem vocali prætextus arundine, Minci!

Sensi equidem gravius carmen.   Nunc cetera pastor

But now my oat proceeds,

And listens to the herald of the sea

That came in Neptune's plea;

He asked the waves, and asked the felon winds,

What hard mishap had doomed this gentle swain?

And questioned every gust of rugged wings,

That blows from off each beaked promontory:

They knew not of his story,

And sage Hippotades their answer brings,

That not a blast was from his dungeon strayed,

The air was calm, and on the level brine

Sleek Panope with all her sisters played.

It was that fatal and perfidious bark

Built in the eclipse, and rigged with curses dark,

That sunk so low that sacred head of thine.

  Next Camus, reverend sire, went footing slow,

His mantle hairy, and his bonnet sedge,

Inwrought with figures dim, and on the edge,

Like to that sanguine flower inscribed with woe.

"Ah! who hath reft," quoth he, "my dearest

      pledge?"

Exsequor. Adstat enim missus pro rege marino,

Seque rogâsse refert fluctus, ventosque rapaces,

Quæ sors dura• nimis tenerum rapuisset agrestem.

Compellasse refert alarum quicquid ab omni

Spirat, acerba sonans, scopulo, qui cuspidis instar

Prominet in pelagus; fama haud pervenerât illuc.

Hæc ultro pater Hippotades responsa ferebat:

"Nulli sunt nostro palati carcere venti.

Straverat æquor aquas, et sub Jove compta sereno

Lusum exercebat Panope nymphæque sorores.

Quam Furiæ struxere per interlunia, leto

Fetam ac fraude ratem,—malos velarat Erinnys,—

Credas in mala tanta caput mersisse sacratum."

Proximus huic tardum senior se Camus agebat;

Cui setosa chlamys, cui pileus ulva: figuris

Idem intertextus dubiis erat, utque cruentos

Quos perhibent flores, inscriptus margine luctum.

"Nam quis," ait, "prædulce meum me pignus

    ademit?"

Last came, and last did go,
The pilot of the Galilean lake.
Two massy keys he bore, of metals twain
(The golden opes, the iron shuts amain).
He shook his mitred locks, and stern bespake:
'' How well could I have spared for thee, young swain,
Enow of such as for their bellies' sake
Creep, and intrude, and climb into the fold!
Of other care they little reckoning make,
Than how to scramble at the shearer's feast,
And shove away the worthy bidden guest;
Blind mouths! that scarce themselves know how
　　　　to hold
A sheep-hook, or have learned aught else the least
That to the faithful herdsman's art belongs!
What recks it them? What need they? They are
　　　　sped;
And when they list, their lean and flashy songs
Grate on their scrannel pipes of wretched straw;
The hungry sheep look up, and are not fed,
But swollen with wind, and the rank mist they draw,
Rot inwardly, and foul contagion spread:
Besides what the grim wolf with privy paw
Daily devours apace, and nothing said.

Post hos, qui Galilæa regit per stagna carinas,

Post hos venit iturus: habet manus utraque
    clavim,

(Queis aperit clauditque) auro ferrove gravatam.

Mitra tegit crines; quassis quibus, acriter infit:

"Scilicet optassem pro te dare corpora leto

Sat multa, o juvenis: quot serpunt ventribus acti,

Vi quot iter faciunt spretis in ovilia muris.

Hic labor, hoc opus est, pecus ut tondente magistro

Præripiant epulas, trudatur dignior hospes.

Capti oculis, non ore! pedum tractare nec ipsi

Norunt; quotve bonis sunt upilionibus artes.

Sed quid enim refert, quove est opus, omnia nactis?

Fert ubi mens, tenue ac deductum carmen avenam

Radit stridentem stipulis. Pastore negato

Suspicit ægra pecus: vento gravis ac lue tracta

Tabescit; mox fœda capit contagia vulgus.

Quid dicam, stabulis ut clandestinus oberrans

Expleat ingluviem tristis lupus, indice nullo?

But that two-handed engine at the door
Stands ready to smite once, and smite no more."
    Return, Alpheus, the dread voice is past,
That shrunk thy streams; return, Sicilian muse,
And call the vales, and bid them hither cast
Their bells and flowerets of a thousand hues.
Ye valleys low, where the mild whispers use
Of shades, and wanton winds, and gushing brooks,
On whose fresh lap the swart star sparely looks,
Throw hither all your quaint enamelled eyes,
That on the green turf suck the honeyed showers,
And purple all the ground with vernal flowers.
Bring the rathe primrose that forsaken dies,
The tufted crow-toe, and pale jessamine,
The white pink, and the pansy freaked with jet,
The glowing violet,
The musk-rose and the well-attired woodbine,
With cowslips wan that hang the pensive head,
And every flower that sad embroidery wears:
Bid amaranthus all his beauty shed,
And daffodillies fill their cups with tears,

Illa tamen bimanus custodit machina portam,

Stricta, paratque malis plagam non amplius unam."

En, Alphee, redi! Quibus ima cohorruit unda

Voces præteriere: redux quoque Sicelis omnes

Musa voca valles; huc pendentes hyacinthos

Fac jaciant, teneros huc flores mille colorum.

O nemorum depressa, sonant ubi crebra susurri

Umbrarum, et salientis aquæ, Zephyrique protervi;

Queisque virens gremium penetrare Canicula parcit:

Picturata modis jacite huc mihi lumina miris,

Mellitos imbres queis per viridantia rura

Mos haurire, novo quo tellus vere rubescat.

Huc ranunculus, ipse arbos, pallorque ligustri,

Quæque relicta perit, vixdum matura feratur

Primula: quique ebeno distinctus, cætera flavet

Flos, et qui specie nomen detrectat eburna.

Ardenti violæ rosa proxima fundat odores;

Serpyllumque placens, et acerbo flexile vultu

Verbascum, ac tristem si quid sibi legit amictum.

To strow the laureate hearse where Lycid lies.

For so to interpose a little ease,

Let our frail thoughts dally with false surmise.

Ay me! whilst thee the shores and sounding seas

Wash far away, where ere thy bones are hurled,

Whether beyond the stormy Hebrides,

Where thou, perhaps, under the whelming tide

Visit'st the bottom of the monstrous world;

Or whether thou, to our moist vows denied,

Sleep'st by the fable of Bellerus old,

Where the great vision of the guarded mount

Looks toward Namancos and Bayona's hold;

Look homeward, angel now, and melt with ruth:

And, O ye dolphins, waft the hapless youth.

Weep no more, woeful shepherds, weep no more,

For Lycidas your sorrow is not dead,

Sunk though he be beneath the watery floor;

So sinks the day-star in the ocean-bed,

And yet anon repairs his drooping head,

Quicquid habes pulcri fundas, amarante: coronent

Narcissi lacrymis calices, sternantque feretrum

Tectus ubi lauro Lycidas jacet: adsit ut oti

Saltem aliquid, ficta ludantur imagine mentes.

Me miserum! Tua nam litus, pelagusque sonorum

Ossa ferunt, queiscunque procul jacteris in oris;

Sive procellosas ultra Symplegadas ingens

Jam subter mare visis, alit quæ monstra profundum;

Sive (negarit enim precibus te Jupiter udis)

Cum sene Bellero, veterum qui fabula, dormis,

Qua custoditi montis prægrandis imago

Namancum atque arces longe prospectat Iberas.

Verte retro te, verte deum, mollire precando:

Et vos infaustum juvenem delphines agatis.

Ponite jam lacrymas, sat enim flevistis, agrestes.

Non periit Lycidas, vestri mœroris origo,

Marmorei quanquam fluctus hausere cadentem.

Sic et in æquoreum se condere sæpe cubile

Luciferum videas; nec longum tempus, et effert

And tricks his beams, and with new-spangled ore
Flames in the forehead of the morning sky :
So Lycidas sunk low, but mounted high,
Through the dear might of him that walked the
    waves,
Where other groves and other streams along,
With nectar pure his oozy locks he laves,
And hears the inexpressive nuptial song,
In the blest kingdoms meek of joy and love.
There entertain him all the saints above,
In solemn troops, and sweet societies,
That sing, and singing in their glory move,
And wipe the tears for ever from his eyes.
Now, Lycidas, the shepherds weep no more;
Henceforth thou art the genius of the shore,
In thy large recompense, and shalt be good
To all that wander in that perilous flood.

   Thus sang the uncouth swain to the oaks and rills,
While the still morn went out with sandals gray.

Demissum caput, igne novo vestitus; et, aurum

Ceu rutilans, in fronte poli splendescit Eoi.

Sic obiit Lycidas, sic assurrexit in altum;

Illo, quem peditem mare sustulit, usus amico.

Nunc campos alios, alia errans stagna secundum,

Rorantesque lavans integro nectare crines,

Audit inauditos nobis cantari Hymenæos,

Fortunatorum sedes ubi mitis amorem

Lætitiamque affert. Hic illum, quotquot Olympum

Prædulces habitant turbæ, venerabilis ordo,

Circumstant: aliæque canunt, interque canendum

Majestate sua veniunt abeuntque catervæ,

Omnibus ex oculis lacrymas arcere paratæ.

Ergo non Lycidam lamentabuntur agrestes.

Divus eris ripæ, puer, hoc ex tempore nobis,

Grande, nec immerito, veniens in munus; opemque

Poscent usque tuam, dubiis quot in æstubus errant.

Hæc incultus aquis puer ilicibusque canebat;

Processit dum mane silens talaribus albis.

He touched the tender stops of various quills,

With eager thought warbling his Doric lay:

And now the sun had stretched out all the hills,

And now was dropped into the western bay;

At last he rose, and twitched his mantle blue,

Tomorrow to fresh woods, and pastures new.

Multa manu teneris discrimina tentat avenis,

Dorica non studio modulatus carmina segni :

Et jam sol abiens colles extenderat omnes,

Jamque sub Hesperium se præcipitaverat alveum.

Surrexit tandem, glaucumque retraxit amictum ;

Cras lucos, reor, ille novos, nova pascua quæret.

IN MEMORIAM.

CVI.

THE time admits not flowers or leaves
    To deck the banquet. Fiercely flies
    The blast of North and East, and ice
Makes daggers at the sharpened eaves,

And bristles all the brakes and thorns
    To yon hard crescent, as she hangs
    Above the wood which grides and clangs
Its leafless ribs and iron horns

Together, in the drifts that pass,
    To darken on the rolling brine
    That breaks the coast. But fetch the wine,
Arrange the board and brim the glass;

IN MEMORIAM.

NON hora myrto, non violis sinit
Nitere mensas. Trux Aquilo foras
 Bacchatur, ac passim pruina
  Tigna sagittifera coruscant;

Horretque saltus spinifer, algidæ
Sub falce lunæ; dum nemori imminet,
 Quod stridet illiditque costis
  Cornua, jam vacuis honorum,

Ferrata; nimbis prætereuntibus,
Ut incubent tandem implacido sali
 Qui curvat oras. Tu Falernum
  Prome, dapes strue, dic coronent.

Bring in great logs and let them lie,
   To make a solid core of heat;
   Be cheerful-minded, talk and treat
Of all things ev'n as he were by:

We keep the day with festal cheer,
   With books and music. Surely we
   Will drink to him whate'er he be,
And sing the songs he loved to hear.

Crateras : ignis cor solidum, graves
Repone truncos. Jamque doloribus
  Loquare securus fugatis
    Quæ socio loquereris illo ;

Hunc dedicamus lætitiæ diem
Lyræque musisque. Illius, illius
  Da, quicquid audit : nec silebunt
    Qui numeri placuere vivo.

LAURA MATILDA'S DIRGE.

FROM 'REJECTED ADDRESSES.'

BALMY Zephyrs, lightly flitting,
    Shade me with your azure wing;
On Parnassus' summit sitting,
    Aid me, Clio, while I sing.

Softly slept the dome of Drury
    O'er the empyreal crest,
When Alecto's sister-fury
    Softly slumb'ring sunk to rest.

Lo! from Lemnos limping lamely,
    Lags the lowly Lord of Fire,
Cytherea yielding tamely
    To the Cyclops dark and dire.

NÆNIA.

O QUOT odoriferi volitatis in aëre venti,
  Cæruleum tegmen vestra sit ala mihi:
Tuque sedens Parnassus ubi caput erigit ingens,
  Dextra veni, Clio: teque docente canam.

Jam suaves somnos Tholus affectare Theatri
  Cœperat, igniflui trans laqueare poli:
Alectûs consanguineam quo tempore Erinnyn,
  Suave soporatam, cœpit adire quies.

Lustra sed ecce labans claudo pede Lemnia linquit
  Luridus (at lente lugubriterque) Deus:
Amisit veteres, amisit inultus, amores;
  Teter habet Venerem terribilisque Cyclops.

K

Clouds of amber, dreams of gladness,

Dulcet joys and sports of youth,

Soon must yield to haughty sadness;

Mercy holds the veil to Truth.

See Erostratus the second

Fires again Diana's fane;

By the Fates from Orcus beckon'd,

Clouds envelop Drury Lane.

Where is Cupid's crimson motion?

Billowy ecstasy of woe,

Bear me straight, meandering ocean,

Where the stagnant torrents flow.

Blood in every vein is gushing,

Vixen vengeance lulls my heart;

See, the Gorgon gang is rushing!

Never, never let us part.

Electri nebulas, potioraque somnia vero;

    Quotque placent pueris gaudia, quotque joci;

Omnia tristitiæ fas concessisse superbæ:

    Admissum Pietas scitque premitque nefas.

Respice! Nonne vides ut Erostratus alter ad ædem

    Rursus agat flammas, spreta Diana, tuam?

Mox, Acheronteis quas Parca eduxit ab antris,

    Druriacam nubes corripuere domum,

· O ubi purpurei motus pueri alitis? o qui

    Me mihi turbineis surripis, angor, aquis!

Duc, labyrintheum, duc me, mare, tramite recto

    Quo rapidi fontes, pigra caterva, ruunt!

Jamque—soporat enim pectus Vindicta Virago;

    Omnibus a venis sanguinis unda salit;

Gorgoneique greges præceps (adverte!) feruntur—

    Sim, precor, o! semper sim tibi junctus ego.

"LEAVES HAVE THEIR TIME TO FALL."

FELICIA HEMANS.

LEAVES have their time to fall,
And flowers to wither at the North-wind's breath,
And stars to set: but all,
Thou hast all seasons for thine own, O Death!

Day is for mortal care,
Eve for glad meetings at the joyous hearth,
Night for the dreams of sleep, the voice of prayer;
But all for thee, thou mightiest of the earth!

The banquet has its hour,
The feverish hour of mirth and song and wine:
There comes a day for grief's overwhelming shower,
A time for softer tears: but all are thine.

"FRONDES EST UBI DECIDANT."

FRONDES est ubi decidant,
Marcescantque rosæ flatu Aquilonio:
   Horis astra cadunt suis;
Sed, Mors, cuncta tibi tempora vindicas.

   Curis nata virûm dies;
Vesper colloquiis dulcibus ad focum;
   Somnis nox magis, et preci:
Sed nil, Terrigenum maxima, non tibi.

   Festis hora epulis datur,
(Fervens hora jocis, carminibus, mero;)
   Fusis altera lacrymis
Aut fletu tacito: quæque tamen tua.

Youth and the opening rose

   May look like things too glorious for decay,

And smile at thee!—but thou art not of those

   That wait the ripen'd bloom to seize their prey!

Virgo, seu rosa pullulans,

Tantum quippe nitent ut nequeant mori?

Rident te?   Neque enim soles

Prædæ parcere, dum flos adoleverit.

"LET US TURN HITHERWARD OUR BARK."

R. C. Trench.

"LET us turn hitherward our bark," they cried,
   "And, 'mid the blisses of this happy isle,
Past toil forgetting and to come, abide
   In joyfulness awhile.

And then, refreshed, our tasks resume again,
   If other tasks we yet are bound unto,
Combing the hoary tresses of the main
   With sharp swift keel anew."

O heroes, that had once a nobler aim,
   O heroes, sprung from many a godlike line,
What will ye do, unmindful of your fame,
   And of your race divine?

"QUIN HUC, FREMEBANT."

"QUIN huc," fremebant, "dirigimus ratem:
Hic, dote læti divitis insulæ,
 Paullisper hæremus, futuri
  Nec memores operis, nec acti:

"Curas refecti cras iterabimus,
Si qua supersunt emeritis novæ:
 Pexisse pernices acuta
  Canitiem pelagi carina."

O rebus olim nobilioribus
Pares: origo Dî quibus ac Deæ
 Heroës! oblitine famæ
  Hæc struitis, generisque summi?

But they, by these prevailing voices now
   Lured, evermore draw nearer to the land,
Nor saw the wrecks of many a goodly prow,
   That strewed that fatal strand;

Or seeing, feared not—warning taking none
   From the plain doom of all who went before,
Whose bones lay bleaching in the wind and sun,
   And whitened all the shore.

Atqui propinquant jam magis ac magis,

Ducti magistra voce, solum : neque

  Videre prorarum nefandas

    Fragmina nobilium per oras;

Vidisse seu non pœnitet—ominis

Incuriosos tot præëuntium,

  Quorum ossa sol siccantque venti,

    Candet adhuc quibus omnis ora.

CARMEN SÆCULARE.

MDCCCLIII.

"Quicquid agunt homines, nostri est farrago libelli."

A CRIS hyems jam venit: hyems genus omne perosa

Fœmineum, et senibus glacies non æqua rotundis:

Apparent rari stantes in tramite glauco;

Radit iter, cogitque nives, sua tela, juventus.

Trux matrona ruit, multos dominata per annos,

Digna indigna minans, glomeratque volumina crurum;

Parte senex alia, prærepto forte galero,

Per plateas bacchatur; eum chorus omnis agrestum

Ridet anhelantem frustra, et jam jamque tenentem

Quod petit; illud agunt venti prensumque resorbent.

Post, ubi compositus tandem votique potitus

Sedit humi; flet crura tuens nive candida lenta,

Et vestem laceram, et venturas conjugis iras:

Itque domum tendens duplices ad sidera palmas,

Corda miser, desiderio perfixa galeri.

At juvenis (sed cruda viro viridisque juventus)

Quærit bacciferas, tunica pendente,* tabernas:

Pervigil ecce Baco furva depromit ab arca

Splendidius quiddam solito, plenumque saporem

Laudat, et antiqua jurat de stirpe Jamaicæ.

O fumose puer, nimium ne crede Baconi:

Manillas vocat; hoc prætexit nomine caules.

Te vero, cui forte dedit maturior ætas

Scire potestates herbarum, te quoque quanti

Circumstent casus, paucis (adverte) docebo.

Præcipue, seu raptat amor te simplicis herbæ,†

Seu potius tenui Musam meditaris avena,

Procuratorem fugito, nam ferreus idem est.

---

* *tunicâ pendente:* h.e. 'suspensâ e brachio.' Quod procuratoribus illis valde, ut ferunt, displicebat. Dicunt vero morem a barbaris tractum, urbem Bosporiam in fl. Iside habitantibus. *Bacciferas tabernas:* id q. nostri vocant "tobacco-shops."

† *herbæ—avend.* Duo quasi genera artis poeta videtur distinguere. 'Weed,' 'pipe,' recte Scaliger.

Vita semiboves catulos, redimicula vita

Candida: de cœlo descendit σῶζε σεαυτόν.

Nube vaporis item conspergere præter euntes

Jura vetant, notumque furens quid femina possit:

Odit enim dulces succos anus, odit odorem;

Odit Lethæi diffusa volumina fumi.

Mille modis reliqui fugiuntque feruntque laborem.

Hic vir ad Eleos, pedibus talaria gestans,

Fervidus it latices, et nil acquirit eundo :*

Ille petit virides (sed non e gramine) mensas,

Pollicitus meliora patri, tormentaque† flexus

Per labyrintheos plus quam mortalia tentat,

Acre tuens, loculisque pilas immittit et aufert.

Sunt alii, quos frigus aquæ, tenuisque phaselus

Captat, et æquali surgentes ordine remi.

---

* *nil acquirit eundo.* Aqua enim aspera, et radentibus parum habilis. Immersum hic aliquem et vix aut ne vix quidem extractum refert schol.

† *tormenta p. q. mortalia.* Eleganter, ut solet, Peile, 'unearthly cannons.' (Cf. Ainsw. D. *s. v.*) Perrecondita autem est quæstio de lusubus illorum temporum, neque in Smithii Dict. Class. satis elucidata. Consule omnino Kentf. de Bill. *Loculis,* bene vertas 'pockets.'

His edura cutis, nec ligno rasile tergum ;

Par saxi sinus : esca boves cum robore Bassi.

Tollunt in numerum fera brachia, vique feruntur

Per fluctus : sonuere viæ clamore secundo :

At piceâ de puppe fremens immane bubulcus

Invocat exitium cunctis, et verbera rapto

Stipite defessis onerat graviora caballis.

Nil humoris egent alii.   Labor arva vagari.

Flectere ludus equos, et amantem devia* currum.

Nosco purpureas vestes, clangentia nosco

Signa tubæ, et caudas inter virgulta caninas.

Stat venator equus, tactoque ferocior armo

Surgit in arrectum, vix auditurus habenam ;

Et jam prata fuga superat, jam flumina saltu.

Aspicias alios ab iniqua sepe rotari

In caput, ut scrobibus quæ sint fastigia quærant ;

Eque rubis aut amne pigro trahere humida crura,

Et fœdam faciem, defloccatumque galerum.

---

* *amantem devia.*   Quorsum hoc, quærunt Interpretes.   Suspicor
equidem respiciendos, vv. 19—23, de procuratoribus.

Sanctius his animal, cui quadravisse rotundum*

Musæ suadet amor, Camique ardentis imago,

Inspicat calamos contracta fronte malignos,

Perque Mathematicum pelagus, loca turbida, anhelat.

Circum dirus "Hymers," nec pondus inutile,

    "Lignum,"

"Salmoque," et pueris tu detestate, "Colenso,"

Horribiles visu formæ; livente notatæ

Ungue omnes, omnes insignes aure canina.†

Fervet opus; tacitum pertentant gaudia pectus

Tutorum; "pulchrumque mori," dixere, "legendo."

Nec vero juvenes facere omnes omnia possunt.

Atque unum memini ipse, deus qui dictus amicis,

Et multum referens de rixatore‡ secundo,

Nocte terens ulnas ac scrinia, solus in alto

Degebat tripode; arcta viro vilisque supellex;

---

* *quadr. rot*ᵐ.—*Cami ard. im*°. Quadrando enim rotundum (Ang. 'squaring the circle') Camum accendere, juvenes ingenui semper nitebantur. Fecisse vero quemquam non liquet.

+ *rure caninâ.* Iterum audi Peile, 'dog's-eared.'

‡ *rixatore.* non male Heins. cum Aldinâ, 'wrangler.'

Et sic torva tuens, pedibus per mutua nexis,

Sedit, lacte mero mentem mulcente tenellam.

Et fors ad summos tandem venisset honores;

Sed rapidi juvenes, queis gratior usus equorum,

Subveniunt, siccoque vetant inolescere libro.

Improbus hos Lector pueros, mentumque virili

Lævius, et duræ gravat inclementia Mortis:*

Suetos (agmen iners), alienâ vivere quadrâ,†

Et lituo vexare viros, calcare caballos.

Tales mane novo sæpe admiramur euntes

Torquibus in rigidis et pelle Libystidis ursæ;

Admiramur opus‡ tunicæ, vestemque‖ sororem

Iridis, et crurum non enarrabile tegmen.

---

* *Mortis.* Verbum generali fere sensu dictum inveni. Suspicor autem poetam virum quendam innuisse, qui currus, caballos, id genus omne, mercede non minimâ locaret.

† *alienâ quadrâ.* Sunt qui de pileis Academicis accipiunt. Rapidiores enim suas fere amittebant. Sed judicet sibi lector.

‡ *opus tunicæ,* 'shirt-work.' Alii *opes.* Perperam.

‖ *vestem.* Nota proprietatem verbi. 'Vest,' enim apud politos id. q. vulgo 'waistcoat' appellatur. Quod et feminæ usurpabant, ut hodiernæ, fibula revinctum, teste Virgilio:

> 'crines nodantur in aurum,
> Aurea purpuream subnectit fibula vestem.'

Hos inter comites implebat pocula sorbis

Infelix puer, et sese recreabat ad ignem,

" Evoe, *Basse," fremens: dum velox præterit ætas;

Venit summa dies; et Junior Optimus exit.

Saucius at juvenis nota intra tecta refugit,

Horrendum ridens, lucemque miserrimus odit:

Informem famulus laqueum pendentiaque ossa

Mane videt, refugitque feri meminisse magistri.

Di nobis meliora! Modum re servat in omni

Qui sapit: haud illum semper recubare sub umbra,

Haud semper madidis juvat impallescere chartis.

Nos numerus sumus, et libros consumere nati;

Sed requies sit rebus; amant alterna Camenæ.

Nocte dieque legas, cum tertius advenit annus:

Tum libros cape; claude fores, et prandia defer.

Quartus venit: ini,† rebus jam rite paratis,

Exultans, et coge gradum conferre magistros.

---

* *Basse.* cft. Interpretes illud Horatianum, "Bassum Threiciâ vincat amystide." Non perspexere viri docti alterum hic alludi, Anglicanæ originis, neque illum, ut perhibent, a potu aversum.

† *Int.* Sic nostri, 'Go in and win.' *rebus,* 'subjects."

His animadversis, fugies immane Barathrum.

His, operose puer, si qua fata aspera rumpas,

Tu rixator eris.   Saltem non crebra revises

Ad stabulum,* et tota mœrens carpere juventa;

Classe nec amisso nil profectura dolentem

Tradet ludibriis te plena leporis HIRUDO.†

---

* *crebra r. a. stabulum.* "Turn up year after year at the old diggings, (*i. e.* the Senate House,) and be plucked," &c.   Peile.   Quo quid jejunius?

+ Classe—Hirudo. Obscurior allusio ad picturam quandam (in collectione viri, vel plusquam viri, Punchii repositam,) in qua juvenis custodem stationis mœrens alloquitur.

TRANSLATIONS FROM HORACE.

TO A SHIP.

Od. i. 14.

YET on fresh billows seaward wilt thou ride,
O ship? What dost thou? Seek a haven, and there
   Rest thee: for lo! thy side
     Is oarless all and bare,

And the swift south-west wind hath maimed thy
      mast,
And thy yards creak, and, every cable lost,
   Yield must thy keel at last
     On tyrannous sea-waves tossed

Too rudely.   Goodly canvas is not thine,

Nor gods, to hear thee, when thy need is sorest :—

   Though thou—a Pontic pine,

     Child of a stately forest—

Boast'st race and idle name, yet little trust

The frightened seamen to the gaudy sail :

   Stay—or become thou must

     The sport of every gale.

Flee—what of late sore burden was to me,

Now a sad memory and a bitter pain,—

   Those shining Cyclads flee

     That stud the far-off main.

TO VIRGIL.

OD. i. 24.

UNSHAMED, unchecked, for one so dear
    We sorrow. Lead the mournful choir,
    Melpomene, to whom thy sire
Gave harp, and song-notes liquid-clear!

Sleeps He the sleep that knows no morn?
    Oh Honour, oh twin-born with Right,
    Pure Faith, and Truth that loves the light,
When shall again his like be born?

Many a kind heart for Him makes moan;
    Thine, Virgil, first. But ah! in vain
    Thy love bids Heaven restore again
That which it took not as a loan:

Were sweeter lute than Orpheus given

    To thee, did trees thy voice obey;

    The blood revisits not the clay

Which He, with lifted wand, hath driven

Into his dark assemblage, who

    Unlocks not fate to mortal's prayer.

    Hard lot! Yet light their griefs who BEAR

The ills which they may not undo.

TO THE FOUNTAIN OF BANDUSIA.

Od. iii. 13.

BANDUSIA, stainless mirror of the sky!
Thine is the flower-crown'd bowl, for thee shall die,
When dawns yon sun, the kid;
Whose horns, half-seen, half-hid,

Challenge to dalliance or to strife—in vain!
Soon must the darling of the herd be slain,
And those cold springs of thine
With blood incarnadine.

Fierce glows the Dog-star, but his fiery beam
Toucheth not thee: still grateful thy cool stream
To labour-wearied ox,
Or wanderer from the flocks:

And henceforth thou shalt be a royal fountain:

My harp shall tell how from yon cavernous mountain,

 Topt by the brown oak-tree,

 Thou breakest babblingly.

SORACTE.

OD. i. 9.

ONE dazzling mass of solid snow
    Soracte stands; the bent woods fret
    Beneath their load; and, sharpest-set
With frost, the streams have ceased to flow.

Pile on great faggots and break up
    The ice : let influence more benign
    Enter with four-years-treasured wine,
Fetched in the ponderous Sabine cup :

Leave to the Gods all else.   When they
    Have once bid rest the winds that war
    Over the passionate seas, no more
Gray ash and cypress rock and sway.

Ask not what future suns shall bring:

 Count to-day gain, whate'er it chance

 To be: nor, young man, scorn the dance,

Nor deem sweet Love an idle thing,

Ere Time thy April youth had changed

 To sourness. Park and public walk

 Attract thee now, and whispered talk

At twilight meetings pre-arranged;

Hear how the pretty laugh that tells

 In what dim corner lurks thy love;

 And snatch a bracelet or a glove

From wrist or hand that scarce rebels.

TO LEUCONÖE.

Od. i. 11.

SEEK not, for thou shalt not find it, what my
    end, what thine shall be;
Ask not of Chaldæa's science what God wills,
    Leuconöe:
Better far, what comes, to bear it. Haply many
    a wintry blast
Waits thee still; and this, it may be, Jove ordains
    to be thy last,
Which flings now the flagging sea-wave on the
    obstinate sandstone-reef.
Be thou wise: fill up the wine-cup; shortening,
    since the time is brief,
Hopes that reach into the future. While I speak,
    hath stol'n away
Jealous Time. Mistrust To-morrow, catch the
    blossom of To-day.

JUNO'S SPEECH.

OD. iii. 3.

THE just man's single-purposed mind
    Not furious mobs that prompt to ill
    May move, nor kings' frowns shake his will
Which is as rock; not warrior winds

That keep the seas in wild unrest;
    Nor bolt by Jove's own finger hurled:
    The fragments of a shivered world
Would crash round him still self-possest.

Jove's wandering son reached, thus endowed,
    The fiery bastions of the skies;
    Thus Pollux; with them Cæsar lies
Beside his nectar, radiant-browed.

For this rewarded, tiger-drawn
    Rode Bacchus, reining necks before
    Untamed; for this War's horses bore
Quirinus up from Acheron.

To the pleased gods had Juno said,
    In conclave: "Troy is in the dust;
    Troy, by a judge accursed, unjust,
And that strange woman prostrated.

"The day Laomedon ignored
    His god-pledged word, resigned to me
    And Pallas ever pure was she,
Her people, and their traitor lord.

"No more the Greek girl's guilty guest
    Sits splendour-girt: Priam's perjured sons
    Find not against the mighty ones
Of Greece a shield in Hector's breast:

"And, long drawn out by private jars,

    The war sleeps. Lo! my wrath is o'er:

    And him the Trojan vestal bore

(Sprung of that hated line) to Mars,

"To Mars restore I. His be rest

    In halls of light: by him be drained

    The nectar-bowl, his place obtained

In the calm companies of the blest.

"While betwixt Rome and Ilion raves

    A length of ocean, where they will

    Rise empires for the exiles still:

While Paris's and Priam's graves

"Are trod by kine, and wild-beasts breed

    Securely there; unharmed shall stand

    Rome's lustrous Capitol, her hand

Curb with proud laws the trampled Mede.

"Wide-feared, to far-off climes be borne
  Her story; where the central main
  Europe and Libya parts in twain,
Where full Nile laves a land of corn:

"The buried secret of the mine
  (Best left there) resolute to spurn,
  Not unto man's base use to turn,
Profane hands laying on things divine.

"Earth's utmost end, where'er it be,
  May her hosts reach; careering proud
  O'er lands where watery rain and cloud,
Or where wild suns hold revelry.

"But, to the warriors of Rome,
  Tied by this law, such fates are willed;
  That they seek never to rebuild,
Too fond, too bold, their grandsires' home.

" With darkest omens, deadliest strife,

    Shall Troy, raised up again, repeat

    Her history; I the victor-fleet

Shall lead, Jove's sister and his wife.

"Thrice let Apollo rear the wall

    Of brass; and thrice my Greeks shall hew

    The fabric down; thrice matrons rue

In chains their sons', their husbands' fall."

Ill my light lyre such notes beseem.

    Stay, Muse; nor, wayward still, rehearse

    The speech of Gods in puny verse

That may but mar a mighty theme.

TO A FAUN.

Od. iii. 18.

WOOER of young Nymphs who fly thee,
 Lightly o'er my sunlit lawn
Trip, and go, nor injured by thee
 Be my weanling herds, O Faun:

If the kid his doomed head bows, and
 Brims with wine the loving cup,
When the year is full; and thousand
 Scents from altars hoar go up.

Each flock in the rich grass gambols
 When the month comes which is thine;
And the happy village rambles
 Fieldward with the idle kine:

Lambs play on, the wolf their neighbour:

  Wild woods deck thee with their spoil;

And with glee the sons of labour

  Stamp upon their foe, the soil.

TO LYCE.

Od. iv. 13.

L YCE, the Gods have listened to my prayer;
The Gods have listened, Lyce. Thou art gray,
   And still wouldst thou seem fair;
    Still unshamed drink, and play,

And, wine-flushed, woo slow-answering Love with
   weak
Shrill pipings. With young Chia he doth dwell,
   Queen of the harp; her cheek
    Is his sweet citadel:—

He marked the withered oak, and on he flew
Intolerant; shrank from Lyce grim and wrinkled,
   Whose teeth are ghastly-blue,
    Whose temples snow-besprinkled:—

Not purple, not the brightest gem that glows,

Brings back to her the years which, fleeting fast,

    Time hath once shut in those

        Dark annals of the Past.

Oh, where is all thy loveliness? soft hue

And motions soft? Oh, what of Her doth rest,

    Her, who breathed love, who drew

        My heart out of my breast?

Fair, and far-famed, and subtly sweet, thy face

Ranked next to Cinara's. But to Cinara fate

    Gave but a few years' grace;

        And lets live, all too late,

Lyce, the rival of the beldam crow:

That fiery youth may see with scornful brow

    The torch that long ago

        Beamed bright, a cinder now.

TO HIS SLAVE.

Od. i. 38.

PERSIAN grandeur I abhor;
Linden-wreathèd crowns, avaunt:
Boy, I bid thee not explore
Woods which latest roses haunt:

Try on nought thy busy craft
Save plain myrtle; so arrayed
Thou shalt fetch, I drain, the draught
Fitliest 'neath the scant vine-shade.

FROM VIRGIL.

THE DEAD OX.

GEORG. IV.

L O! smoking in the stubborn plough, the ox
Falls, from his lip foam gushing crimson-stained,
And sobs his life out. Sad of face the swain
Moves, disentangling from his comrade's corpse
The lone survivor: and its work half-done,
Abandoned in the furrow stands the plough.
Not shadiest forest-depths, not softest lawns,
May move him now: not river amber-pure,
That rolls from crag to crag unto the plain.
Powerless the broad sides, glazed the rayless eye,
And low and lower sinks the ponderous neck.
What thank hath he for all the toil he toiled,
The heavy-clodded land in man's behoof

Upturning? Yet the grape of Italy,

The stored-up feast hath wrought no harm to him:

Green leaf and taintless grass are all their fare;

The clear rill or the travel-freshen'd stream

Their cup: nor one care mars their honest sleep.

FROM THEOCRITUS.

THE GOATHERD.

IᴛᴅLL VII.

SCARCE midway were we yet, nor yet descried

The stone that hides what once was Brasidas:

When there drew near a wayfarer from Crete,

Young Lycidas, the Muses' votary.

The horned herd was his care: a glance might tell

So much: for every inch a herdsman he.

Slung o'er his shoulder was a ruddy hide

Torn from a he-goat, shaggy, tangle-haired,

That reeked of rennet yet: a broad belt clasped

A patched cloak round his breast, and for a staff

A gnarled wild-olive bough his right hand bore.

Soon with a quiet smile he spoke—his eye

Twinkled, and laughter sat upon his lip:

" And whither ploddest thou thy weary way

Beneath the noontide sun, Simichides?

For now the lizard sleeps upon the wall,

The crested lark hath closed his wandering wing.

Speed'st thou, a bidden guest, to some reveller's
    board?

Or townward, to the treading of the grape?

For lo! recoiling from thy hurrying feet

The pavement-stones ring out right merrily."

FROM SOPHOCLES.

SPEECH OF AJAX.

Soph. *Aj.* 645.

ALL strangest things the multitudinous years

Bring forth, and shadow from us all we know.

Falter alike great oath and steeled resolve;

And none shall say of aught, 'This may not be.'

Lo! I myself, but yesterday so strong,

As new-dipt steel am weak and all unsexed

By yonder woman: yea I mourn for them,

Widow and orphan, left amid their foes.

But I will journey seaward—where the shore

Lies meadow-fringed—so haply wash away

My sin, and flee that wrath that weighs me down.

And, lighting somewhere on an untrodden way,

I will bury this my lance, this hateful thing,

Deep in some earth-hole where no eye shall see—

Night and Hell keep it in the underworld!

For never to this day, since first I grasped

The gift that Hector gave, my bitterest foe,

Have I reaped aught of honour from the Greeks.

So true that byword in the mouths of men,

"A foeman's gifts are no gifts, but a curse."

    Wherefore henceforward shall I know that God

Is great; and strive to honour Atreus' sons.

Princes they are, and should be obeyed.   How else?

Do not all terrible and most puissant things

Yet bow to loftier majesties?   The Winter,

Who walks forth scattering snows, gives place anon

To fruitage-laden Summer; and the orb

Of weary Night doth in her turn stand by,

And let shine out, with her white steeds, the Day:

Stern tempest-blasts at last sing lullaby

To groaning seas: even the arch-tyrant, Sleep,

Doth loose his slaves, not hold them chained for

      ever.

And shall not mankind too learn discipline?
I know, of late experience taught, that him
Who is my foe I must but hate as one
Whom I may yet call Friend: and him who loves
     me
Will I but serve and cherish as a man
Whose love is not abiding. Few be they
Who reaching Friendship's port, have there found
     rest.

  But, for these things, they shall be well. Go thou,
Lady, within, and there pray that the Gods
May fill unto the full my heart's desire.
And ye, my mates, do unto me with her
Like honour: bid young Teucer, if he come,
To care for me, but to be your friend still.
For where my way leads, thither I shall go:
Do ye my bidding: haply ye may hear,
Though now is my dark hour, that I have peace.

FROM LUCRETIUS.

Book II.

SWEET, when the great sea's water is stirred
    to his depths by the storm-winds,
Standing ashore to descry one afar-off mightily
    struggling:
Not that a neighbour's sorrow to you yields dulcet
    enjoyment;
But that the sight hath a sweetness, of ills our-
    selves are exempt from.
Sweet 'tis too to behold, on a broad plain mustering,
    war-hosts
Arm them for some great battle, one's self un-
    scathed by the danger:—
Yet still happier this:—To possess, impregnably
    guarded,

Those calm heights of the sages, which have for
    an origin Wisdom;

Thence to survey our fellows, observe them this
    way and that way

Wander amidst Life's paths, poor stragglers seeking
    a highway:

Watch mind battle with mind, and escutcheon rival
    escutcheon;

Gaze on that untold strife, which is waged 'neath
    the sun and the starlight,

Up as they toil on the surface whereon rest Riches
    and Empire.

    O race born unto trouble! O minds all lacking
    of eyesight!

'Neath what a vital darkness, amidst how terrible
    dangers,

Move ye thro' this thing, Life, this fragment! Fools,
    that ye hear not

Nature clamour aloud for the one thing only; that,
    all pain

Parted and past from the Body, the Mind too bask
in a blissful

Dream, all fear of the future and all anxiety over!
Now, as regards Man's Body, a few things only
are needful,

(Few, tho' we sum up all,) to remove all misery
from him;

Aye, and to strew in his path such a lib'ral carpet
of pleasures,

That scarce Nature herself would at times ask
happiness ampler.

Statues of youth and of beauty may not gleam
golden around him,

(Each in his right hand bearing a great lamp
lustrously burning,

Whence to the midnight revel a light may be
furnishèd always);

Silver may not shine softly, nor gold blaze bright,
in his mansion,

Nor to the noise of the tabret his halls gold-
    cornicèd echo :—

Yet still he, with his fellow, reposed on the velvety
    greensward,

Near to a rippling stream, by a tall tree canopied
    over,

Shall, though they lack great riches, enjoy all
    bodily pleasure.

Chiefliest then, when above them a fair sky smiles,
    and the young year

Flings with a bounteous hand over each green
    meadow the wild-flowers :—

Not more quickly depart from his bosom fiery fevers,

Who beneath crimson hangings and pictures
    cunningly broidered

Tosses about, than from him who must lie in
    beggarly raiment.

Therefore, since to the Body avail not Riches,
    avails not   N

Heraldry's utmost boast, nor the pomp and the pride
    of an empire;
Next shall you own, that the Mind needs likewise
    nothing of these things.

Unless—when, peradventure, your armies over the
    champaign
Spread with a stir and a ferment, and bid War's
    image awaken,
Or when with stir and with ferment a fleet sails
    forth upon Ocean—
Cowed before these brave sights, pale Superstition
    abandon
Straightway your mind as you gaze, Death seem
    no longer alarming,
Trouble vacate your bosom, and Peace hold holiday
    in you.

But, if (again) all this be a vain impossible
    fiction;
If of a truth men's fears, and the cares which hourly
    beset them,

Heed not the jav'lin's fury, regard not clashing
    of broadswords;

But all-boldly amongst crowned heads and the rulers
    of empires

Stalk, not shrinking abashed from the dazzling
    glare of the red gold,

Not from the pomp of the monarch, who walks forth
    purple-apparelled:

These things shew that at times we are bankrupt,
    surely, of Reason;

Think too that all Man's life through a great Dark
    laboureth onward.

For, as a young boy trembles, and in that mystery,
    Darkness,

Sees all terrible things: so do we too, ev'n in the
    daylight,

Ofttimes shudder at that, which is not more really
    alarming

Than boys' fears, when they waken, and say some
    danger *is* o'er them.

So this panic of mind, these clouds which gather
    around us,
Fly not the bright sunbeam, nor the ivory shafts
    of the Day-star:
Nature, rightly revealed, and the Reason only,
    dispel them.

Now, how moving about do the prime material
    atoms
Shape forth this thing and that thing; and, once
    shaped, how they resolve them;
What power says unto each, This must be; how an
    inherent
Elasticity drives them about Space vagrantly on-
    ward;
I shall unfold: thou simply give all thyself to my
    teaching.
Matter mingled and massed into indissoluble
    union

Does not exist. For we see how wastes each
    separate substance;

So flow piecemeal away, with the length'ning cen-
    turies, all things,

Till from our eye by degrees that old self passes,
    and is not.

Still Universal Nature abides unchanged as afore-
    time.

Whereof this is the cause. When the atoms part
    from a substance,

That suffers loss; but another is elsewhere gaining
    an increase:

So that, as one thing wanes, still a second bursts
    into blossom,

Soon, in its turn, to be left. Thus draws this
    Universe always

Gain out of loss; thus live we mortals one on
    another.

Bourgeons one generation, and one fades. Let but
    a few years

Pass, and a race has arisen which was not: as in
     a racecourse,
One hands on to another the burning torch of
     Existence.

*   *   *   *   *   *   *

FROM HOMER.

Il. I.

SING, O daughter of heaven, of Peleus' son, of
    Achilles,

Him whose terrible wrath brought thousand woes
    on Achaia.

Many a stalwart soul did it hurl untimely to Hades,

Souls of the heroes of old: and their bones lay
    strown on the sea-sands,

Prey to the vulture and dog. Yet was Zeus ful-
    filling a purpose;

Since that far-off day, when in hot strife parted
    asunder

Atreus' sceptred son, and the chos'n of heaven,
    Achilles.

  Say then, which of the Gods bid arise up battle
    between them?

Zeus's and Leto's son. With the king was kindled

his anger:

Then went sickness abroad, and the people died

of the sickness:

For that of Atreus' son had his priest been lightly

entreated,

Chryses, Apollo's priest. For he came to the ships

of Achaia,

Bearing a daughter's ransom, a sum not easy to

number:

And in his hand was the emblem of Him, far-

darting Apollo,

High on a sceptre of gold : and he prayed to the hosts

of Achaia;

Chiefly to Atreus' sons, twin chieftains, ordering

armies.

" Chiefs sprung of Atreus' loins; and ye, brazen-

greavèd Achaians!

So may the Gods this day, the Olympus-palacèd,

grant you

Priam's city to raze, and return unscathed to your
  homesteads :

Only my own dear daughter I ask ; take ransom
  and yield her,

Rev'rencing His great name, son of Zeus, far-
  darting Apollo."

  Then from the host of Achaians arose tumultuous
  answer :

" Due to the priest is his honour ; accept rich
  ransom and yield her."

But there was war in the spirit of Atreus' son,
  Agamemnon ;

Disdainful he dismissed him, a right stern fiat
  appending :—

  " Woe be to thee, old man, if I find thee lingering
  longer,

Yea or returning again, by the hollow ships of
  Achaians !

Scarce much then will avail thee the great god's
  sceptre and emblem.

Her will I never release.   Old age must first come
    upon her,

In my own home, yea in Argos, afar from the land
    of her fathers,

Following the loom, and attending upon my bed.
    But avaunt thee!

Go, and provoke not me, that thy way may be haply
    securer."

  These were the words of the king, and the old
    man feared and obeyed him:

Voiceless he went by the shore of the great dull-
    echoing ocean,

Thither he gat him apart, that ancient man; and a
    long prayer

Prayed to Apollo his Lord, son of golden-ringleted
    Leto:

  "Lord of the silver bow, thou whose arm girds
    Chryse and Cilla,—

Cilla beloved of the Gods,—and in might sways
    Tenedos, hearken!

Oh! if, in days gone by, I have built from floor
    unto cornice,

Smintheus, a fair shrine for thee; or burned in the
    flames of the altar

Fat flesh of bulls and of goats; then do this thing
    that I ask thee:

Hurl on the Greeks thy shafts, that thy servant's
    tears be avengèd!"

    So did he pray, and his prayer reached the ears
    of Phœbus Apollo.

Dark was the soul of the god as he moved from the
    heights of Olympus,

Shouldering a bow, and a quiver on this side fast
    and on that side.

Onward in anger he moved. And the arrows,
    stirred by the motion,

Rattled and rang on his shoulder: he came as
    cometh the midnight.

Hard by the ships he stayed him, and loosed one
shaft from the bow-string;

Harshly the stretched string twanged of the bow
all silvery-shining.

First fell his wrath on the mules, and the swift-.
footed hound of the herdsman;

Afterward smote he the host. With a rankling
arrow he smote them

Aye; and the morn and the even were red with
the glare of the corpse-fires.

Nine days over the host sped the shafts of the
god: and the tenth day

Dawned; and Achilles said, "Be a council called
of the people."

(Such thought came to his mind from the goddess,
Hera the white-armed,

Hera who loved those Greeks, and who saw them
dying around her.)

So when all were collected and ranged in a solemn
assembly,

Straightway rose up amidst them and spake swift-
footed Achilles :—

"Atreus' son! it were better, I think this day,
that we wandered

Back, re-seeking our homes, (if a warfare *may* be
avoided);

Now when the sword and the plague, these two
things, fight with Achaians.

Come, let us seek out now some priest, some seer
amongst us,

Yea or a dreamer of dreams—for a dream too cometh
of God's hand—

Whence we may learn what hath angered in this
wise Phœbus Apollo.

Whether mayhap he reprove us of prayer or of
oxen unoffered;

Whether, accepting the incense of lambs and of
blemishless he-goats,

Yet it be his high will to remove this misery from
us."

Down sat the prince: he had spoken. And
uprose to them in answer

Kalchas Thestor's son, high chief of the host of
the augurs.

Well he knew what is present, what will be, and
what was aforetime:

He into Ilion's harbour had led those ships of
Achaia,

All by the Power of the Art, which he gained from
Phœbus Apollo.

Thus then, kindliest-hearted, arising spake he before
them:

"Peleus' son! Thou demandest, a man heaven-
favour'd, an answer

Touching the Great King's wrath, the afar-off
  aiming Apollo:

Therefore I lift up my voice. Swear thou to me,
  duly digesting

All,—that with right good will, by word and by
  deed, thou wilt aid me.

Surely the ire will awaken of one who mightily
  ruleth

Over the Argives all: and upon him wait the
  Achaians.

Aye is the battle the king's, when the poor man
  kindleth his anger:

For, if but this one day he devour his indignation,

Still on the morrow abideth a rage, that its end
  be accomplished,

Deep in the soul of the king. So bethink thee,
  wilt thou deliver."

　　Then unto him making answer arose swift-
  footed Achilles:

"Fearing naught, up and open the god's will, all
that is told thee:

For by Apollo's self, heaven's favourite, whom thou,
Kalchas,

Serving aright, to the armies aloud God's oracles
op'nest:

None—while as yet I breathe upon earth, yet walk
in the daylight—

Shall, at the hollow ships, lift hand of oppression
against thee,

None out of all your host—not and if thou nam'st
Agamemnon,

Who now sits in his glory, the topmost flower of
the armies."

Then did the blameless prophet at last take
courage and answer:

"Lo! He doth not reprove us of prayer or of oxen
unoffered;

But for his servant's sake, the disdained of king
    Agamemnon,

(In that he loosed not his daughter, inclined not
    his ear to a ransom,)

Therefore the Far-darter sendeth, and yet shall send
    on us, evil.

Nor shall he stay from the slaughter the hand
    that is heavy upon you,

Till to her own dear father the bright-eyed maiden
    is yielded,

No price asked, no ransom ; and ships bear hallowèd
    oxen

Chryse-wards :—then, it may be, will he shew
    mercy and hear us."

  These words said, sat he down. Then rose in
    his place and addressed them

Atreus' warrior son, Agamemnon king of the
    nations,

Sore grieved.   Fury was working in each dark cell
of his bosom,

And in his eye was a glare as a burning fiery
furnace :

First to the priest he addressed him, his whole
mien boding a mischief.

" Priest of ill luck !   Never heard I of aught
good from thee, but evil.

Still doth the evil thing unto thee seem sweeter
of utt'rance ;

Leaving the thing which is good all unspoke, all
unaccomplished.

Lo! this day to the people thou say'st, God's oracles
op'ning,

What, but that *I* am the cause why the god's hand
worketh against them,

For that in sooth I rejected a ransom, ay and
a rich one,

Brought for the girl Briseis. I did. For I chose
> to possess her,
Rather, at home: less favour hath Clytemnestra
> before me,
Clytemnestra my wife: unto her Briseis is equal,
Equal in form and in stature, in mind and in
> womanly wisdom.
Still, even thus, am I ready to yield her, so it be
> better:
Better is saving alive, I hold, than slaying a
> nation.
Meanwhile deck me a guerdon in her stead, lest of
> Achaians
I should alone lack honour; an unmeet thing and
> a shameful.
See all men, that my guerdon, I wot not whither
> it goeth."

Then unto him made answer the swift-foot
> chieftain Achilles:

"O most vaunting of men, most gain-loving, off-
    spring of Atreus!

How shall the lords of Achaia bestow fresh guerdon
    upon thee?

Surely we know not yet of a treasure piled in
    abundance!

That which the sacking of cities hath brought tc
    us, all hath an owner,

Yea it were all unfit that the host make re-
    distribution.

Yield thou the maid to the god.   So threefold
    surely and fourfold

All we Greeks will requite thee, should that day
    dawn, when the great gods

Grant that of yon proud walls not one stone rest
    on another."

       *   *   *   *   *

"COME LIVE WITH ME."

COME live with me and be my love,
And we will all the pleasures prove
That valleys, groves, or hill or field,
Or woods or steepy mountains yield.

And we will sit upon the rocks,
Seeing the shepherds feed their flocks
By shallow rivers, to whose falls
Melodious birds sing madrigals.

And I will make thee beds of roses
And a thousand fragrant posies:
A gown made of the finest wool,
Which from our pretty lambs we'll pull.

"ET NOS CEDAMUS AMORI."

TRANSFER amantis amans laribus te, Delia,
    nostris;
Ruris ut innumeras experiamur opes:
Quot vallis, juga, saltus, ager, quot amœna ministrat
    Mons gravis ascensu, suppositumve nemus.

Scilicet acclines scopulo spectare juvarit
    Ducat uti pastum Thyrsis herile pecus,
Ad vada rivorum; queis adsilientibus infra,
    Concordes avibus suave loquantur aves.

Ipse rosas, queis fulta cubes caput, ipse recentum
    Quidquid alant florum pascua mille, feram:
Pro læna tibi vellus erit, neque tenuior usquam,
    Me socio teneras quo spoliaris oves.

The shepherd swains shall dance and sing
For thy delight each May morning:
If these delights thy mind may move,
Come live with me and be my love.

MARLOW.

If all the world and love were young,
And truth in every shepherd's tongue,
These pretty pleasures might me move
To live with thee and be thy love.

Time drives the flocks from field to fold,
When rivers rage, and rocks grow cold;
And Philomel becometh dumb;
The rest complain of cares to come.

But could youth last and love still breed,
Had joys no date nor age no need,
Then these delights my mind might move
To live with thee and be thy love.

RALEIGH.

Cantabunt salientque tibi pastoria pubes,

    Maia novum quoties jusserit ire diem :

Quæ si forte tibi sint oblectamina cordi,

    Te laribus nostris transfer, amantis amans.

Finge nec huic mundo nec amoribus esse senectam ;

    Pastorumque labris usque subesse fidem :

His ducta illecebris (est his sua namque venustas)

    Deliciæ forsan dicerer usque tuæ.

Sed pecus it tandem campis in ovile relictis ;

    Sævit ubi fluvius, saxaque frigus habet ;

Cessat ubi Philomela loqui ; stantque agmina ramis

    Cetera, curarum questa quod instat onus.

Fac semper subolescat amor superetque juventus ;

    Gaudia fac careant fine, senecta malis ;

Atque ego—quam perhibes dulcedine subdita pectus—

    Deliciæ tempus dicar in omne tuæ.

"POOR TREE."

POOR tree; a gentle mistress placed thee here,
  To be the glory of the glade around.
Thy life has not survived one fleeting year,
  And she too sleeps beneath another mound.

But mark what differing terms your fates allow,
  Though like the period of your swift decay:
Thine are the sapless root and wither'd bough;
  Hers the green memory and immortal day.

CARLISLE.

FLEBILIS ARBOR.

TE dominæ pia cura solo, miseranda, locarat
    Patentis, arbor, ut fores agri decus.
At mansit tua vita brevem non amplius annum;
    At ipsa dormit extero sub aggere.
Quam diversa tamen sors est (adverte) duarum!
    Fugax utramque vexit hora; sed tibi,
Arbor, truncus iners, frons arida restat: at illi
    Perenne lumen ac virens adhuc amor.

Idem aliter redditum.

Mollis huc hera quam tulit caducam
    Ut saltus decus, arbor, emineres,
Anno non superas brevi peracto;
    At cespes procul ambit arctus illam.
Pares funere (dispares eædem
    Quanto discite) marcuistis ambæ.
Frons restat tibi passa, sicca radix;
    Illi lux nova jugiter virenti.

*** *The five following translations were made for "Hymns Ancient and Modern, with some Metrical Translations," etc., published* 1867.

XLIV.—CHRISTMAS.

LANIGEROS, acclinis humo, pastoria pubes
    Custodiebat dum greges ;
Splendescente polo longe lateque, Jehovæ
    Descendit ales nuncius.
Qui " Quid" ait " tremitis"—namque anxia pectora
    terror
    Immanis occupaverat—
"Grata fero : magnum jubeo lætarier et vos
    Et quicquid est mortalium.
Namque in Davidis urbe, satus quoque Davidis idem
    E stirpe, jamjam nascitur
Vestra Salus, Dominus vester, cognomine Christus ;
    Signoque vobis hoc erit :

venietur ibi cælestis scilicet Infans,
  Spectabiturque jam viris;
scia velarit meritum non talia corpus,
  Condente præsepi caput."

ixerat ales. Eo simul apparere videres
  Dicente lucentem chorum
rce profectorum supera; pæanaque lætum
  His ordiebantur modis:
Qui colit alta Deo summi tribuantur honores,
  Virisque pax arrideat;
rotenus excipiat cæli indulgentia terras,
  Haud dirimenda sæculis."

cxxx.—PENTECOST.

CÆLO profecti vis et ira nuntiæ
   Fuere quondam Numinis :
Nimbos secantis pedibus; instar ignium
   Hac parte, nigros altera.

At prodeunti vis amorque denuo
   Ibant ministri; mollius
Sacer Palumbes dimovebat aera
   Quam mane primo flamina.

Quot occuparant impetu flammæ fero
   Arcem Sinai, suaviter
Tot consecratum nunc in omne defluunt
   Caput, corona nobilis.

Ac vox uti prægrandis arrectas metu,
   Ut clangor aures perculit,
(Cælestium quo cœtus audito tremunt,)
   E nocte trepidans nubium;

Sic prodeunte Spiritu Dei suos,

    Ut pastor, inventum greges,

Late sonabat vox, profecta cælitus,

    Tumultuosi turbinis.

Templum Jehovæ quâ, scatetque criminum

    Fecundus orbis undique;

In pervicaci scilicet demum sinu

    Desideratura locum.

Huc, Numen adsis! Vis, Amor, Prudentia,

    Adsis ut aures audiant;

Bene ominatum quisque captet ut diem

    Amore sospes an metu.

CXXXIX.

QUI pretium nostræ vitam dedit, ante ' Supremum
    Valete' quam vix edidit,
Solamenque Ducemque viris legarat eundem,
    Quo contubernales forent.
Venit at Ille suæ partem dulcedinis ultro
    Ut hospes efflaret bonus,
Nactus ubi semel esset, amat qua sede morari,
    Casti latebras pectoris.
Hinc illæ auditæ voces, qualemque susurrum
    Nascente captes Vespero;
Quo posuere metus, patitur quo frena libido,
    Spirare viso cælitus.
Ac virtutis inest si quid tibi, si quid honorum
    Claro triumphis contigit;
Venerit in mentem si quid divinius unquam;
    Hæc muneris sunt Illius.

t candens, at mite veni nunc, Numen, opemque

    Nostræ fer impotentiæ;

ɔr nunc omne domus pateat tua; feceris omne

    Cor incola te dignius.

osque Patrem, Natum vos tollite; neve recuses

    Tu sancte laudem Spiritus:

ignus enim tolli, Tria qui Deus audit in Uno,

    Unumve malit in Tribus.

CXCVII.

AUXILIUM quondam, nunc spes, Deus, unica
    nostri;
Flaute noto portus, præteritoque domus:
Gens habitat secura tuæ tua sedis in umbra;
    Simus ut incolumes efficit una manus.
Terræ olim neque forma fuit neque collibus ordo:
    Tu, quot eunt anni, numen es unus idem.
Sæcla vides abiisse, fugax ut vesper; ut actis
    Quæ tenebris reducem prorogat hora diem.
*Stant populi, ceu mane novo juga florea, quorum
    Marcidus ad noctem falce jacebit honos:
*Tu "suboles terrena, redi" nec plura locuto,
    Quippe satæ gentes pulvere pulvis erunt.
Quos genuit, secum rotat usque volubilis ætas;
    Ut sopor in cassum, luce solutus, eunt.

Tu quondam auxilium, spes nunc, Deus, ultima

nostri,

Sis columen trepidis, emeritisque domus.

---

* Two stanzas are translated here which do not appear in the received editions of *Hymns Ancient and Modern.* They are quoted as part of this hymn by Miss Brontë in *Shirley*, and run as follows :

> "Thy word commands our flesh to dust—
> 'Return, ye sons of men;'
> All nations rose from earth at first,
> And turn to earth again.

> "Like flowery fields the nations stand,
> Fresh in the morning light;
> The flowers beneath the mower's hand
> Lie withering ere 'tis night!"

Possibly Miss Brontë quoted from memory, and the true version of the first stanza may be—

> All nations rose from earth, and must
> Return to earth again.

CCXX.

QUO chaos ac tenebræ quondam fugere locuto,
  Supplicis, Omnipotens, accipe vota chori:
Quaque jubar nondum micuit quod sole, quod astris
  Clarius est, dicas "Exoriare dies!"
Qui dignatus eras descendere more sequestri
  Alitis ad terram, luxque salusque virûm;
Ægro mente salus, lux interioris egeno
  Luminis: at tòto jam sit in orbe dies!
Unde fides, amor unde venit; qui Spiritus audis;
  Carpe, dator vitæ, sancte Palumbes, iter:
Incubet ætherios spargens tua forma nitores
  Fluctubus, ut terræ lustret opaca dies!
Quique, Triplex, splendes tamen integer; ipse vicissim
  Robur, Amor, Virtus; usque beate Deus:
Quale superbit aquis indignaturque teneri
  Fine carens pelagus, crescat ubique dies!

ccxlii.—DEDICATION OF A CHURCH.

VERBUM superni Numinis
Qui cuncta comples, hanc domum
Amore certo consecres
Et feriatis annuas.

E fonte pueros hoc fluit
In criminosos gratia;
Beata cogit unctio
Nitere nuper sordidos.

Hic Christus animis dat cibo
Corpus suum fidelibus;
Cælestis agnus proprii
Fert ipse calycem sanguinis.

Hinc venia mœstis ac salus
Reis emenda; dum favet
Judex, et ingens gratia
Scelere sepultos integrat.

Hic, regnat alte qui Deus,

Benignus habitat; hic pium

Pectus gubernat atria

Desiderantum cælica.

In dedicatam trux domum

Procella nequidquam furit;

Atrox eo vis Tartari

Passura fertur dedecus.

At robur, at laus tibi, Pater,

Sit comparique Filio;

Diique amoris vinculo,

Dum sæcla currunt, Flamini.

J. PALMER, PRINTER, CAMBRIDGE.

By the same Author.

TRANSLATIONS INTO ENGLISH and LATIN.
Crown 8vo. 7*s*. 6*d*.

THEOCRITUS TRANSLATED INTO ENGLISH
VERSE. Crown 8vo. 7*s*. 6*d*.

DEIGHTON, BELL, AND CO., CAMBRIDGE.

CPSIA information can be obtained
at www.ICGtesting.com
Printed in the USA
LVHW102049171022
730905LV00004B/394